"You said we were going to take this a step at a time."

"It's the first one, I guess." Wade released a rough breath. "Or maybe the second. We might've skipped one somewhere."

Bailey clung dizzily to him. "What are we supposed to do now?"

"That's up to you. If it was up to me, I'd kiss you all night."

"Just kiss?" She touched her lips softly to his.

He held her tighter. "You're teasing me."

"I'm teasing myself, too." She was lost in the moment. "Come to my room with me, Wade."

He released her. "Are you sure? Because you're the one who said that if we go too far, there'll be no turning back."

"Yes, but we both know that we won't be lovers forever." She skimmed a hand down his chest. "We can just be together for now."

* * *

Out of the Friend Zone by Sheri WhiteFeather is part of the LA Women series.

Dear Reader,

I wanted to take this opportunity to thank you for your friendship and support over the years. My first book came out in 1999, and many of you have been with me every step of the way. I've enjoyed getting to know you on social media and receiving your cards, emails and letters. Some of you are around my age, and some of you were teenagers and young adults when we first connected. It's been a pleasure watching all of you grow and change. I wish each and every one of you much love and joy.

As always, I hope you enjoy this book. It's the second story in my LA Women series featuring a couple who met in high school and are now falling *Out of the Friend Zone* and becoming lovers.

Hugs and happy reading,

Sheri WhiteFeather

SHERI WHITEFEATHER

OUT OF THE FRIEND ZONE

Recycling programs for this product may not exist in your area.

ISBN-13: 978-1-335-73557-7

Out of the Friend Zone

Copyright © 2022 by Sheree Henry-Whitefeather

This edition published by arrangement with Harlequin Books S.A.

For questions and comments about the quality of this book, please contact us at CustomerService@Harlequin.com.

Harlequin Enterprises ULC
22 Adelaide St. West, 41st Floor
Toronto, Ontario M5H 4E3, Canada
www.Harlequin.com

Printed in U.S.A.

Sheri WhiteFeather is an award-winning bestselling author. She lives in Southern California and enjoys shopping in vintage stores and visiting art galleries and museums. She is known for incorporating Native American elements into her books and has two grown children who are tribally enrolled members of the Muscogee Creek Nation. Visit her website at www.sheriwhitefeather.com.

Books by Sheri WhiteFeather

Harlequin Desire

Sons of Country

Wrangling the Rich Rancher
Nashville Rebel
Nashville Secrets

Daughters of Country

Hot Nashville Nights
Wild Nashville Ways

LA Women

Hollywood Ex Factor
Out of the Friend Zone

Visit her Author Profile page at Harlequin.com, or www.sheriwhitefeather.com, for more titles.

You can also find Sheri WhiteFeather on Facebook, along with other Harlequin Desire authors, at Facebook.com/harlequindesireauthors!

One

Bailey Mitchell glanced around the crystal ballroom at the famed Beverly Hills Hotel, with its Art
Deco decor and stunning architecture. The ballroom
was packed with her peers, and to the untrained eye,
Bailey probably seemed cool and collected, dressed
in a chic little black dress with her long blond hair
coiled in a trendy updo. Yet on the inside, she was
so nervous she could barely breathe.

This posh event was her fifteen-year high school
reunion, and although she was a successful thirty-
three-year-old screenwriter with strong opinions, she
felt like a teenager who was about to be bullied all
over again. Her stupid name badge wasn't helping,

either. She'd always hated her senior picture, and now she wore it stuck to her chest.

Was she the only alumna who'd come here alone? Or just the only one who felt so alone? She wished her bestie, Margot, could've made it, but she was out of town and wouldn't be back until tomorrow. Thankfully, Margot would be available for the second day of the reunion, a picnic at Griffith Park. But tonight Bailey was flying solo.

She'd told herself that she had to attend the gathering. She wanted to face the past, to show the jerks who'd bullied her that she wasn't going to cower in a corner. But now that she was here, she was actually standing in a corner, sipping a glass of chardonnay all by herself. Granted, she'd only just arrived, and this was still the cocktail hour. But would she find the gumption to socialize? To stick around for the dinner and dancing that would round out the rest of the festivities?

Of course she would. If she didn't, she would never forgive herself. She just hoped that she didn't trip over her words when she opened her mouth. Sometimes she stuttered when she got nervous. It had started in high school, during the bullying, and had been categorized as stress-related. She'd gotten plenty of therapy for it, but in high-anxiety situations, it still sneaked up on her.

She scanned the crowd, looking for Wade Butler. His name was on the guest list, so she already knew that he'd confirmed to be here. Aside from Margot,

Wade had been her only salvation in high school. Back then he'd been a reclusive boy who'd gotten bullied, too. A brilliant computer genius who'd come to Bailey's rescue whenever he saw someone picking on her. Wade wasn't your typical tech nerd. He used to shroud himself in a long black coat and combat boots, looking more goth than geek. Other kids at other schools dressed that way, too. That style had always been around. But at their preppy academy, it had seemed out of sync. Of course, there'd been so much more to Wade than his rebellious appearance. He'd gotten arrested their senior year for hacking into the FBI and the accessing their files. He'd actually solved some of their cyber division crimes, which was what he'd set out to do. Only the FBI wasn't impressed with his effort, at least not back then. Since Wade had been eighteen at the time—an adult, not a juvenile—he'd spent five years in a federal prison. These days, he was a software developer, computer security consultant and public speaker. A big-time tech billionaire. Talk about turning your life around. Even the FBI used him as one of their consultants now.

Bailey hadn't seen him since the day he'd gotten hauled away in handcuffs, but recently, in the weeks leading up to the reunion, she'd checked him out online. She'd also read a feature on him in *Entrepreneur* magazine. As far as she could tell—from his pictures, anyway—his appearance had changed. He'd traded in his oversize coat and combat boots for designer suits. Fifteen years later, Wade Butler was downright dashing.

She kept scanning the ballroom, looking for him. There were lots of polished men here. Beverly West Academy, or Bev West, as it was known, was one of the top-rated private schools in Los Angeles, and most of their graduating class had come from money, including Bailey. Wade had been neither rich nor poor. He'd been one of the in-betweens, students whose families had to make financial sacrifices to send their kids there. Not that she knew much about Wade's family, other than that his mother had passed away before he'd come to Bev West, leaving him in the care of his stepfather.

But, overall, Wade had rarely talked about himself. Sometimes he used to join her and Margot for lunch, but mostly he sat off by himself, way out on the grass, his nose buried in his laptop. They never saw him outside school, either.

Suddenly Bailey felt someone come up behind her, working themselves into the corner where she stood. She sensed a male presence. Was it one of the boys who'd tried to date her just so they could meet her sex-symbol mom? Most of her tormentors had been girls. But lots of boys had shamed her, too.

Refusing to let anyone get the best of her now, she spun around and came face-to-face with Wade.

He smiled, and she nearly melted to the floor. He'd always been tall, but the boyish lankiness was gone. His body had filled out, and his features had grown stronger and sharper, creating handsome edges and mysterious angles. His light brown hair was slicked back in a stylish, classy way, but it was his eyes that demanded attention: gray with flecks of green. She remembered them well. Sometimes they even changed color, going from gray to green.

"Hey, Bailey," he said. "Long time no see."

"Hi, Wade." She struggled to catch her breath. He wore a sleek black suit and a diamond-encrusted watch. He had a glass in his hand, full of a clear liquid—vodka maybe, or silver tequila. "I'm glad you're here."

"You, too." He scanned the length of her, apparently appreciating what he saw. "You look amazing, by the way."

"Thank you. You grew up good, too." She didn't know what else to say. She'd had a swirly little crush on him back in the day, and history was repeating itself. "How have you been?"

"Besides getting reformed and all that? I've been hanging in there." He shrugged. "I hope they don't put my mug shot on the slideshow, though. That wasn't exactly my finest hour."

"In that case, I hope they don't put up that awful picture Shayla Lewis took of me. The one she emailed to her friends so they could forward it to whoever they wanted." Nowadays it would have been through texts, but emails had been more common then. In the picture, Bailey been changing in gym, bending over, with the crack of her butt exposed through her panties. "My face wasn't in it, but Shayla made sure that everyone knew it was me." Bailey winced, the pain from the past digging into her. "Why am I telling you this? You must have seen it."

Wade frowned. "No, I didn't. No one ever sent it to me."

"You could've hacked into Shayla's computer to get a glimpse." That would have been a simple task for him—a lot easier than the FBI stunt he'd pulled.

"I would never be party to something that was humiliating to you like that."

She went warm, touched by his words, by the gentleness in his eyes. "Thanks. You didn't miss much. I'm not a pinup, not like my mom." But that was the whole point. Bailey had gotten bullied because her ultrafamous actress mother had been considered one of the sexiest women in the world, the MILF of all MILFs, and Bailey had been her shy and awkward daughter.

Wade shifted his stance. "Is Shayla Lewis here tonight? If she is, you ought to take a compromising picture of her and send it around."

"She's here. I noticed her when I picked up my name tag. She's on the committee that helped organize the reunion."

He glanced toward the center of the ballroom, where many of their former classmates were gathered. "I don't see her. Is she old and ugly now, with lots of warts?"

Bailey laughed at his deadpan expression. "Unfortunately, she's as attractive as ever. The last I heard, she and her husband founded a successful men's fashion line."

"Remind me never to wear any of their stuff." He moved a bit closer to her. "Why are we hiding out here instead participating in the cocktail hour?"

"I do have a cocktail." She sipped her wine, making a show of it. "You have one, as well."

"That's true. I guess we can still be each other's prom date from this cozy corner."

Did that mean she could kiss him good night? She'd always wanted to kiss him, even when they were young. "In case you haven't noticed, this is our reunion, not the prom."

"Yeah, I missed that event. Did you go?"

She shook her head. "I missed it, too." But she hadn't been in federal prison, so his excuse was better than hers. "No one asked me, but I didn't want to go, anyway." She hesitated. "Before we join the party for real, there's something I want to run past you. A nonprofit I've been working on."

He raised his eyebrows. "Are you hitting me up for a donation?"

"Yes, I am. But what can I say? Your reputation for philanthropy precedes you." She'd read about all the good he'd done in the world. "I'd be remiss not to hit you up. But I also thought I should do it before we face the people who used to bully us."

"Why? Is your charity an antibullying organization?"

"Actually, it is. It's called the Free Your Heart Foundation. I'm creating an online forum where people can share their stories, connect with others who are going through a tough time or apologize to anyone, past or present, that they might've hurt. I plan to open an education center, too, and organize in-person events where bullied kids can get together for a safe space."

"Of course I'll donate. I'd be glad to help drum up other donors, too, if you'd like."

"Thank you. That would be wonderful. I appreciate your support." She felt her pulse spike. Being around him was intoxicating. "Are you attending the picnic tomorrow? Maybe we can talk more about it then."

"Sure, we can do that. Initially, I wasn't planning on going, but I can meet you there. I can't stay the whole time, though. I live in the Bay Area now, and I'm flying home tomorrow. I left LA a long time ago."

"I'm still here. I live in Laurel Canyon. And I was aware that you'd moved. Your online profiles list San Francisco as your home." In a section of Pacific Heights known as Billionaire's Row, she thought. He'd made it to the very top of the world, with other tech giants as his neighbors.

He checked out the ballroom again, and Bailey followed his line of sight. Even as adults, the popular crowd still stuck together. The homecoming queen wore a paper crown that someone had jokingly plunked on her head, her former court surrounding her, laughing and talking.

Wade asked, "Have you discussed your nonprofit with the reunion committee? Do they know what you've got brewing?"

"No. But I haven't told my story publicly yet. I plan to write an essay about my experiences as soon the foundation launches. Not all of the details. Some of it I'd rather keep private. But for now, I'm just trying to be brave by coming here." She paused to collect her thoughts. "Just so you know, your charitable nature isn't the only reason I wanted to see you again. I also wanted to reconnect and remember you for the hero you were to me in high school. You're the only one who ever defended me." He'd even jumped Randall Kincaid, a vulgar-mouthed boy who'd been taunting her. He'd shoved Randall against a locker, an act that had culminated in a fight. For a skinny kid, Wade had packed a mean punch. "You got a two-week suspension over me."

"My stepdad was mad about that. He worried about how the suspension was going to affect my college admissions. But I was okay with staying home. It gave me more time to plan The Outlaw's next move."

Bailey went silent, imagining him in that role. The Outlaw was his teenage alter ego and the name he'd given himself when he was hacking into the FBI and bragging about his crime-solving antics on an anonymous blog he'd created.

"I can't tell you how shocked all of us were when we found out that was you," she said. By then, The Outlaw's legend had grown to epic proportions. "Some of the people who bullied you were fans of The Outlaw, and they didn't have a clue that the hacker they'd been admiring was you."

"No one put it together, except the federal agents who eventually caught up with me. But it doesn't matter now." Wade swigged his drink. "I'm not that guy anymore."

"Do you still have the computer code tattoo on your wrist? Or did you have it removed?" She couldn't tell since he was wearing long sleeves, but she recalled how unusual it was.

He lifted his arm, the diamonds on his watch catching the light. "It's under here." He gazed at her short black dress. "You don't have any hidden tattoos, do you?"

She shook her head. But now she wished that her entire body was inked, just so she could show him. Suddenly, she got the devilish urge to take him home tonight, straight to her bed.

Seriously? She was having *those* kinds of thoughts? As a rule, Bailey didn't have mindless flings. Overall, she didn't do much of anything. She'd only had a few lovers, choosing her partners wisely. Bailey had always been sensible about sex, but now she wanted to get reckless with Wade.

"I think we should enter the lion's den," he said. "The buffet is going to open soon. The DJ is setting up his equipment, too. Music from our youth, no doubt."

She struggled to clear her mind, to stop thinking about doing wicked things with him. "A playlist we'll all remember."

"Exactly." He extended his arm. "Shall we go?"

She linked her arm through his, still fighting forbidden feelings. She'd never even fulfilled her teenage fantasy of kissing him, yet here she was, wanting him in the most intimate of ways.

Wade enjoyed watching Bailey eat. She'd overfilled her plate at the buffet, and he suspected that her eyes were bigger than her stomach. But he also noticed how precise she was, sampling each entrée with the finesse of a food critic.

They sat at a table with a group of former students who'd been decent to them, the type who'd focused on their studies and avoided confrontation. The clique who'd hurt them was on the other side of the room, making lots of noise and taking tons of selfies. He'd never really understood why they'd picked on Bailey. Why did it matter that her mother was a Hollywood bombshell? Half of their school was connected to that industry. Sure, Bailey had been a quiet girl, a daydreamer, he supposed. But she'd grown up as rich and privileged as the rest of them. By most standards, that alone should've gotten her off the hook. Yet people like Shayla Lewis and Randall Kincaid had gone to great lengths to destroy her, even causing her to stutter. He remembered how she used to struggle to speak around them.

To Wade, Bailey had always been beautiful. All that long blond hair and those big blue eyes. He was still captivated by her.

She had the right idea by creating an antibullying organization and channeling her energy into something positive. Mostly Wade tried to do that, too. But coming back to LA and reliving his youth was weighing on him. Not just the bullying, but the family secret that he kept bottled up inside.

At one time, he'd been a seemingly normal kid. But after his mom died and he'd learned the truth about his dad, he'd become a dark and brooding outcast, withdrawing into himself. By then, he was walking around in a daze and getting harassed for being "weird." His only escape had been hiding behind his computer and morphing into The Outlaw.

He leaned closer to Bailey and whispered, "I have a confession to make. I did hack into Shayla's computer."

She blinked at him. "You looked at my picture?"

"No. But I messed with some of her files. I even deleted her term papers. I thought she deserved it after what she did to you."

"Oh my goodness, Wade." Bailey put down her fork and reached over to put her hand against his cheek. "I appreciate that you were thinking of me, but two wrongs don't make a right."

"I know, but it was The Outlaw who did it, and

he was still on a crime spree." He covered her hand with his, excited to be touching her.

Their gazes met and held. Other people at their table were talking, but Wade could barely hear them now, their voices fading into the background. The dinner music the DJ was playing was drifting away, too. At the moment, Wade's only focus was Bailey. He'd wanted to be with her in high school, but he'd been too insecure to ask her out. Maybe he could date her now? Thing was, he didn't do relationships. His idea of dating was discreet affairs. Something detached, something private. And he couldn't begin to guess if that was Bailey's style. He moved his hand away from hers.

She returned to her meal. But a second later, she asked, "Do you like mushrooms?"

"Why?" He gazed at the spinach-stuffed portobello she was cutting into. "Is that the kind that makes a person hallucinate?"

She laughed. "I hope not. Or I'm going to be stoned out of my mind. I've eaten two of these already. I just thought that if you liked mushrooms, you should try them. I noticed that you don't have any on your plate."

"I like mushrooms just fine."

"I can let you have this one." She brought a bite up to his mouth. "Careful, it's still hot."

Not as hot as her feeding him. He took a bite of the mushroom in question. He chewed and swallowed. She fed him a bit more, and she kept giving it to him until it was gone. By the time he was finished, he imagined that he'd just had a hot and hungry affair with the girl of his boyhood dreams.

"Good?" she asked.

"Yeah, good." Wade shook off the feeling. He had no business letting his mind go there.

To keep himself sane, he reached for his napkin and tuned back into the music. Green Day's "Boulevard of Broken Dreams" was playing. A song about loneliness. Was that an omen?

"This was my anthem in high school," Bailey said.

"It was mine, too." He must've listened to it hundreds of times, alone in his room with his blackout curtains drawn tight. His stepdad, a business operations manager named Carl, hated those drapes and was always bugging him to let the sun in. In the end, it was Carl who'd told Wade the truth about his dad.

Bailey sighed. "We had a lot in common back then."

Aside from being bullied, he wasn't sure that was true. Not unless she had skeletons in her closet. But once this trip down memory lane was over, Wade could slam the door on his past and quit thinking about it. He'd done everything within his power to protect his secret, and he wasn't going to let it come barreling back to haunt him. He wanted to enjoy getting to know Bailey again.

She glanced at him from beneath her lashes, and he swigged his water. He liked the way the loose strands of her hair tumbled around her face. Most of it was piled on her head and twisted into a deliberately messy bun. To him, it made her look as if she'd just gotten out of bed, except for the fancy barrettes on the sides. He couldn't tell if they were helping hold the bun in place or were just for decoration. He wouldn't mind removing them to find out. Maybe he would ask her to dance later—fast, slow, it didn't matter. He just wanted an excuse to get closer.

"I was surprised that you came here alone," he said. "I expected Margot Jensen to be with you. You were always together at school, and I saw on your Instagram that she's engaged to your brother. Or remarrying him or whatever."

She gave him a humored look. "You cyberstalked me and my family?"

"I didn't stalk anyone. I just scrolled through your pictures. I figured it was a good way to see what you've been up to before you and I got reacquainted."

She cocked her head. "Why didn't you just follow me?"

"I could ask you the same thing. You aren't following me, either, but you've poked around on my social media, too." She'd already mentioned the information she'd gleaned from his online profiles. "But it's no big deal. People look each other up all the time."

"True, but you probably socialize with the wizards who created those sites. I'm just a regular user who gets confused whenever the formats change."

Her honesty made him smile. "The next time

you're confused, you can call me and I'll walk you through the changes." He figured that was a clever way of offering her his number.

She accepted it, programming it into her phone and giving him her number, too. If they'd been able to do that in high school, they might've actually dated. But would a romance have improved their situation? Or made it more complicated?

While his mind drifted uncomfortably back to the past, he said, "I wonder if I should tell Shayla that I messed with her computer when I was The Outlaw."

"Whatever for?" Bailey asked.

"Because of what you said about two wrongs not making a right." He frowned, disturbed by his memories. "I wanted so badly to protect your honor, but I shouldn't have stooped to Shayla's level."

"She doesn't appear to be sorry for what she did to me. Or at least she hasn't shown that side of herself. I know a lot more about the psychology of bullying now than I did when we were young, and I suspect that there was something in her background that caused her behavior."

"It's tough to say what made her so cruel. But I thought that everything I was doing was for the greater good. I claimed to be a white-hat hacker. But I fell into a gray area. Not just with what I did to Shayla, but with the FBI, too. I exposed their vulnerabilities by bragging about how easily I got into their system. It's funny, too, because when they arrested me, I still didn't see the harm in my actions. I thought they should've been grateful that I'd solved some of their cyber division crimes."

"They appreciate you now." She smiled a little. "You're one of the top consultants in your field. Maybe I should write a screenplay about you."

His heart banged against his ribs. The last thing he needed was for Bailey to go poking around in his life. "You'd be wasting your time. No one would want to see a movie about me."

"I think you'd make an interesting subject, but I'd never write it without your input."

Then it was never going to happen, he thought. He'd be damned if he would run the risk of being exposed. It was bad enough that his dad's victims had already been featured on a newsmagazine show, with a mystery about who'd reimbursed the money that had been swindled from them.

Bailey glanced down at her plate. "I took too much food. There's no way I can finish this. Do you want some more of it?"

"No, thanks." He doubted that she was going to feed him again. "I've got plenty of my own."

They continued eating until the music stopped, and Bailey's shoulders tensed.

"What's going on?" Wade asked.

She gestured to the stage. "They're getting ready to do the slideshow, and look who's getting up to announce it."

Wade watched Shayla head for the podium, gliding across the floor like the belle of the ball. "Doesn't that figure? I'll bet she nominated herself for the job."

"She's always been the master of ceremonies."

"Yeah, well, before this night is over, I'm going to talk to her, not just to admit what I did to her, but to let her know that I haven't forgotten what she did to you, either."

"You're going to speak on my behalf?"

"I was hoping that you'd join me. Having you there might motivate her to apologize or at least show some sort of remorse. She owes you that much."

Bailey sucked a bit of air between her teeth. "It is an interesting idea, us approaching her together."

"Damn straight, it is. We didn't come here to blend into the background." He looked into her eyes. "We came here to be strong. You and me, all smart and sexy and grown-up."

Two

Bailey loved Wade's description of them. *All smart and sexy and grown-up.* It definitely made them sound strong.

She studied him, watching how the candlelight, reflected off the glittering centerpiece on the table, played across his face. "Thank you for saying that." The sexy part made her a little woozy, though. It almost made them seem like lovers. "That's a phrase I'm never going to forget."

He smiled, and she nearly got lost in those gray-green eyes. But before she got carried away, staring too deeply at him, she turned her attention to the stage, where Shayla asked the student body president to join her for the presentation.

Soon after that, the cheerleaders were corralled. They gathered in a row, dressed in their party clothes. When they chanted one of their old cheers, the room erupted into claps and silly laughter.

Once the cheerleaders departed, Shayla returned to the stage, taking the spotlight again.

Wade was right, Bailey thought. At some point tonight, they needed to approach Shayla and kick-start a conversation with her. She wasn't the only bully in attendance, but she'd been the ringleader, the one who'd cast herself in the mean-girl role, encouraging other people to do hurtful things, too. Whatever the psychology behind it was, Shayla hadn't lost her superior edge, and Bailey was still feeling the brunt of having been torn apart by her.

Finally, the slideshow began. Bailey was fairly certain that neither she nor Wade would be included. But Bailey wasn't likely to forget the half-naked picture Shayla had taken of her, and neither, she suspected, was anyone else. Things like that stayed in people's minds.

Wade reached for her hand, and about fifteen minutes later, the presentation ended. Bailey hadn't been part of it. But she'd actually spotted a shot of Wade, far away in the background, behind a group of other kids, the hem of his signature coat flapping in the wind.

She leaned toward him. "Did you see yourself? You looked like a superhero compared to the rest of them."

"That's what I always wanted to be," he replied. "That coat was my cape. My cloak of invisibility."

She understood what he meant. The coat had made him look like a desperado, flaunting the outlaw he'd become without anyone even knowing it. "You were hiding in plain sight."

"I most definitely was." He shifted in his chair. "Should we go say hello to Shayla now?" He gestured with the tilt of his head. "She's back at her table now."

An instant fear crept up Bailey's spine. What if she wasn't as smart and sexy and grown-up as Wade had said? What if she stuttered when she tried to talk to Shayla?

No, she thought. She wasn't going to freak herself out and start behaving like an anxious teenager all over again. She was a successful screenwriter now, a woman who shouldn't be intimidated by the past. But regardless of how far she'd come, she was still battling a case of nerves.

"Will you start the dialogue?" she asked Wade.

"Absolutely," he reassured her. "We got this, Bailey."

They walked across the ballroom together. A majority of guests remained at their tables, while others flocked to the dessert bar. Smokers headed outside to light up or vape. No one was dancing, as the dance floor hadn't opened up yet. The DJ was on a break.

Shayla saw them coming. Her gaze darted in their direction, but only for a second. She held her head high, this tall, slim brunette who'd been one of the most fashionable girls in school. She used to brag about being the heiress to a luxury department store empire, a chain that was on the verge of bankruptcy now. But even so, she hadn't let her family's struggles deter her. She'd married well and started her own successful company. Bailey tried not to wish ill on other people, but it irked her that Shayla managed to maintain her social status.

Wade strolled right over to Shayla, and she got up from her seat. Bailey stood next to Wade, taking calculated breaths.

"We just wanted to say hello," he said to Shayla. "And to congratulate you and your committee for doing such a great job with the reunion."

"Thank you." Shayla seemed surprised. Clearly, she hadn't expected Wade to compliment her. With a quick frown, she appeared to be taking in his classic haircut, his custom-tailored suit, his jeweled watch. She didn't seem to like that he'd gotten so rich, either, that the boy who'd gone to prison had become a billionaire. At least there was some vindication in that, Bailey thought.

"So," Wade said, "where's Randall Kincaid?"

"He wasn't able to make it," Shayla replied.

"Is he still recovering from the fat lip I gave him?" Wade asked with a slight smile and dry wit.

Shayla's laugh sounded strained. "I think Randall is away on business, but one never really knows."

"No, one doesn't. But I need to clear the air about

something." Wade spoke in a cool, calm voice. "I hacked into your computer during high school. I messed with some of your files and deleted your term papers."

"That was you?" Shayla gaped at him. "I thought it was some sort of malware. I had no idea that someone, that you—"

"I'm sorry I did it. Truly I am. It wasn't right. But I'm not the only one who did things back then that they should be sorry for."

Oh, wow, Bailey thought. Wade wasn't holding back, not in the least. But Shayla wasn't taking the bait, either. She just stood there like a stone. No recognition of her actions. No apology. No nothing. She acted as if she'd never done a thing.

Refusing to let it end there, Bailey joined the conversation. She moved forward and said to Shayla, "I'm starting an antibullying foundation, a nonprofit that's near and dear to my heart. I'd be glad to send you some information about it."

Shayla fidgeted with the rubies at her ears. "Oh, I see." Her expression remained stoic. "If you're looking for donations, you can reach me through the contact information I left on the reunion site." She put her hand on the back of a chair, where a dark-haired man sat, his back to them. Her husband, no doubt. But he wasn't paying any attention to them. He didn't even turn around.

"I'll be in touch with the specifics," Bailey said. "Then you can decide what you want to do." She glanced at Wade, letting him know that she was done talking to the bully who'd tormented her.

He nodded, and they walked away. He took her hand, and she realized how easily she was getting used to being touched by him.

"See? That wasn't so bad," he said. "We said our piece and left her with some things to think about."

"Do you think she'll donate?" Bailey wasn't the least bit sure of Shayla. "Or do you think she just said that to get us to leave her alone?"

"It's impossible to know what she'll do. But guess what? The DJ is back, and we're just in time to dance." He paused. "Will you dance with me?"

"Yes, of course. But if we go now, we'll be the first people out there."

"Personally, I'd rather make a statement by being the first. But if you're not comfortable doing that, we can go back to our table and wait."

No, she thought. After their private showdown with Shayla, they needed to be seen, to make a statement, to show the Class of 2007 how bold they were. "Let's do it. Let's lead the way."

He escorted her onto the dance floor, and the DJ played a slow song, a soft rock ballad from their junior year.

Wade took Bailey in his arms, and they swayed to the beat. At this point, she didn't care how many people watched them, or talked about them, or remembered how shy or strange they used to be. She looked up at Wade, and he gazed down at her. The heat be-

tween them was palpable. She could feel it everywhere, all over her body, in her blood, in her bones.

"I used to imagine dancing with you," he said.
"It was one of my fantasies. But I didn't have the
courage to take you out for a burger, let alone to a
school dance."

"I had fantasies about you, too." She still did. Fantasies about taking him home, about being more sex-
ually adventurous than she'd ever been in her whole
cautious little life.

The second song was another ballad, so they
stayed locked in each other's arms. The dance floor
began to fill up, and soon they were immersed in
a sea of people. But somehow, it still seemed as if
they were alone.

Within no time, as the music got faster, the party
got moving. Bailey spun around, free as a bird,
bumping and grinding and getting deliberately
naughty. Wade was making some moves, too. But
what choice did they have? The DJ was on a roll,
playing songs from the era of their misspent youth.

She couldn't begin to guess how long they danced.
But when they stopped, she was as thirsty as sin.
Wade retrieved two icy glasses of sparkling water
from the bar. She drank hers so fast, the bubbles
tickled all the way to her toes.

They went outside to get some air and sat on a
bench in the courtyard. Bailey was glad that she'd
worn her hair up. Otherwise it would have been
sticking to her skin.

"That was fun," she said, leaning back against the bench. "But I should have taken off my shoes. I don't do heels very often. I'm more of a flats and sneakers kind of gal."

"You can take them off now." He shot her a playful grin. "You can take off anything you want."

"Is this dangerous?" she asked. "What we're doing?"

He looked confused. "What do you mean?"

"You and me, flirting and acting like we own the place."

"It's only dangerous if we let it go to our heads. And we'll both be better behaved at the picnic tomorrow."

She glanced up at the stars. It was a pretty summer night, bright and clear. "I've always been better behaved. I didn't even lose my virginity until I was in my twenties."

"Really? Me, neither." He frowned. "But I was locked up until then."

"And no one hurt you when you were in prison?" She'd heard stories about the horrible things that happened to inmates.

"No. At least not in that way. It was a minimum-security facility. There weren't any violent offenders there. Still, I learned really fast how to survive and protect myself. I wasn't taking any chances."

"I've thought a lot about you over the years." Her heart pounded harder. "I probably shouldn't say this, but I've been imagining taking you home with me tonight."

He stared at her. "Is that an invitation?"

"I don't know." Her thoughts had gone fuzzy. "I just know that it keeps popping into my mind."

"Maybe it's just another fantasy, like when we were young."

"It definitely is. But I probably shouldn't act on it, no matter how exciting it would be."

His breathing went rough. "Is it easier now that you mentioned it? That you got it out of the way?"

"And decided not to do it?" She hoped so, but she couldn't be sure. At the moment, nothing seemed easy. "If it had been an invitation, would you have accepted?"

"In the heat of the moment, I definitely would've." He hesitated. "But we barely know each other anymore, and things like that can get complicated."

"That's why I'm careful who I sleep with." Sometimes she created sultry characters in her screenplays, but her own life wasn't nearly as provocative.

Wade smoothed his hair, taming the strands that had fallen forward when he'd been dancing. "Do you want to pig out on dessert?"

"As a substitute for sex?" She smiled in spite of herself. "I might eat everything in sight."

"That's the idea," he quipped.

She agreed to give it a try, and they returned to the ballroom, preparing to immerse themselves in mounds of sugar.

* * *

Everything at the dessert bar looked pretty damned good. Going home with Bailey would've been better, Wade thought, only that wasn't an option.

After they made their selections, they looked around for a place to sit, agreeing not to occupy the same table as before. Instead, they found a secluded spot near the exit, as if both of them were already searching for an escape.

"I'm going to get a drink," he said. "Can I get you something?"

"I'll take a cup of coffee with extra cream."

He stood with his back to the dance floor, but he could still feel the vibration of the music. "Decaf or regular?"

"Regular." She dipped into a frothy Neapolitan mousse. "Then I can be on a sugar and caffeine high."

Wade hadn't decided what to drink; he just knew alcohol would be involved. But he would get her beverage first. The coffee and tea were self-serve.

As he crossed the room, his thoughts strayed, and he imagined what sleeping with Bailey would be like. He envisioned all sorts of scenarios.

Silky warmth. Desperate surrender. Hot, hard lust.

He cursed his unruly mind and reached the beverage station. He poured Bailey's coffee, then gathered a handful of packaged creamers and a stir stick.

He returned to their table and placed everything in front of her. "I'll be right back." He dashed off to the bar, anxious for his drink.

When it came time for him to order, he went for a Baileys Irish Cream. If he couldn't have the woman, then he was going to try to satisfy himself with a whiskey liqueur of the same name.

He tasted it and imagined that he was tasting her. Damn, but his libido was out of whack, using alcohol in place of a person. But that was what the desserts were for, too.

He rejoined Bailey. She'd finished her mousse and was going after a pink macaron.

"What'd you get?" she asked, pointing to his drink.

He didn't want to admit what it was, at least not outright, so he shrugged and said, "Just something I was in the mood for." He lifted a lemon bar off his plate and examined it, realizing how cowardly it was to evade her question. "Actually, it's Baileys Irish Cream."

Her eyes went wide. "Should I be flattered?"

"Most definitely. You inspired it."

In the silence that followed, he bit into the lemon bar, and she nibbled on her macaron.

As he watched her lick some cookie crumbs from her lips, he asked, "Did you know that there's difference between macaroons and macarons? Macaroons are made with coconut, and macarons are made with meringue. I learned that from my chef."

"You have a private chef? We had one when I was growing up. My mother still does, but I prefer to cook for myself now."

"Are you good with breakfast?" A second later, he added, "I love it when women bring me breakfast in bed." He couldn't seem to stop himself from saying it.

"Is your chef a woman?" she asked, angling her head at him. "If she is, then you can have her bring you breakfast in bed anytime you want."

"My chef is a man. My personal assistant is a guy. My pilot is a dude, too."

"Are there any women who work for you?"

"My art dealer is female. And so is my tailor. I also have a lady barber." He leaned forward in his chair, closer to her. "Have I ever told you how much I like your hair? Is it still as long as it used to be?"

"It's longer now." She toyed with one of loose tendrils framing her face. "It goes all the way to my tailbone. Or the longest part does. It's cut in layers."

He sipped his liqueur, letting the whiskey flow through him. "Will you wear it loose at the picnic tomorrow? I'd like to see it that way."

"I hardly ever wear it down." She released an audible breath. "But I'm not sure if I should be taking hairstyle requests from you. Or talking about breakfast in bed or any of this."

"You're right." He winced at his blunders. "We're supposed to be repressing our appetite for each other, not exacerbating it."

She sighed. "It's okay. I'm just as guilty as you are. I'm the one who started this whole thing. I never should've told you that I had that type of interest in you."

"I think it's better that you did. Or we'd be fighting it even more than we already are." He smiled a bit a foolishly. "Is the sugar and caffeine helping?"

"Not necessarily." She flashed a silly smile, too. "How's the Baileys working for you?"

"I'll let you know when I'm in bed, all by my lonesome tonight." He raised his glass and downed the rest of it. "I'm staying at this hotel in one of their grand deluxe suites."

"Great, now I can picture where you're sleeping. But a little imagination never hurt anyone, I guess."

He had lots of imagination when it came to her. Too much, he supposed. Distracting himself, he took a quick survey of the crowd. "It's quieter now. People are starting to leave."

"I'm not ready to go." Her gaze locked onto his. "I like being here with you, even if I shouldn't be enjoying it as much as I am."

"Do you want to dance again? The music is slow." The lights were lower, too. "Things are definitely quieting down."

"Then let's soak it up before it's over. But this time I'm taking off my shoes." She stood and removed her heels.

He liked that she was barefoot. It made her look soft and natural. "You're such a tiny little thing."

"The correct word for a woman who is small in stature is *petite*." She teased him with a smile. "Just in case you want to rephrase your description of me."

"Really? You're correcting my grammar? I ought to scoop you up and carry you out onto the dance floor, just to show how easily I can toss you over my shoulder, like the *tiny little thing* that you are."

She lifted her chin. "You wouldn't dare."

Was she challenging him? "Don't tempt me. Because I will go caveman on you."

She laughed and made a mad dash for the dance floor. He chased after her, caught her with one arm and drew her tight against him. He didn't pick her up. They were dancing now, immersed in a tender moment.

He slid his hand down her spine. He wanted to kiss her, right here and now. But he kept his urges to himself. Otherwise he might end up in her bed, where he wasn't supposed to be. Or she might succumb and join him in his. His room was closer. Just an elevator ride away.

"Let's stay to the end," he said. If he couldn't be with her all night, then the least he could do was make the dancing last. "Until the final song."

She swayed to the music. "Have you listened to the lyrics of this one? It's about the ravages of love."

"Lots of songs are. That's a common theme. I've never felt that way about anyone."

"Neither have I." She gazed up at him. "I think falling in love would hurt."

"I think so, too." His mother had loved his father, and that relationship had brought nothing but destruction. "I don't ever want to experience it."

She put her head on his shoulder. "Me, neither."

In most cases, he would've thought this was an odd conversation. But with her, it seemed to make sense. A boy and a girl, he thought. A man and a woman. Two long-ago crushes at their high school reunion, analyzing grown-up feelings.

A short time later, they danced to the last song, along with a few other stragglers. Mostly everyone was gone, even the people on the reunion committee. But they were probably gearing up for tomorrow's event.

Wade and Bailey returned to their table so she could get her shoes. He watched her slip them on.

"Can I walk you out to the valet?" he asked.

"Actually, you can walk me directly to my car. I didn't valet park. I was too nervous when I first got here to get caught up with everyone else who was arriving."

They didn't speak as they headed to the parking structure. Everything seemed eerily quiet now.

Finally, when they were on the level where she'd parked, he asked, "What are you driving?"

"A 1956 F-100. It was my dad's, and he left it to me when he passed away. It's fully restored."

Wade turned and saw it. It couldn't be missed. The truck was an explosion of shiny black paint and polished chrome. "That's a sweet ride."

"Thank you. It's not my everyday truck. I have a newer one, too. But it's not nearly as flashy. What about you?"

He studied her. She was fishing around in her bag for her keys. "For this trip, I'm using a car service."

She glanced up. "I meant, what do you drive when you're at home?"

"I have lots of cars. I switch off, depending on my mood."

"Do you do that with women, too?"

He raised his eyebrows. "Are you accusing me of being a player?"

She jangled her keys. "No. But that doesn't mean you don't jump from lover to lover."

"I'm cautious about my affairs." She'd already told him how careful she was, and now he was copping to the same guarded behavior. "I don't jump into anything."

"That's good to know." She moved closer to her truck. "But we probably shouldn't be talking about this. Except that I brought it up again, didn't I?" She shook her head. "Why do I keep doing that?"

He shrugged, feigning a joke. "Because you find me irresistible, I guess."

"I'm resisting you just fine." She sounded worried, far too uncertain. "If I wasn't, I wouldn't be going home alone."

He longed to press her against that spiffy black Ford and let all hell break loose. But he crammed his hands in his pockets, making damned sure that he kept his distance. "Text me when you get to the park tomorrow, and we'll meet up."

"I will. Margot and my brother and her son are going, too. We can all hang out." She unlocked the door, climbed into the cab and rolled down the manual window. When she started the engine, the truck roared to life. "Sleep well, Wade."

"You, too." He stepped back, wired as hell. Sleep was going to be a long time coming.

Three

Bailey got up early and drove to the beach where Margot lived with Bailey's brother, Zeke, and Margot's adoptive son, Liam. Margot and Zeke had a complex relationship. Currently, they were engaged, but they'd been married to each other before. After the divorce, they'd started having a sex-only affair, and now they were together again and planning their second wedding.

Love was strange, Bailey thought. She'd never understood it. But she was happy for Margot and Zeke. And Liam, too. They were a great family.

She arrived at their house, a gorgeous glass structure that overlooked the Pacific Ocean. They'd closed escrow on it about a month ago. Prior to that, they'd been living in separate residences and bouncing back and forth.

Bailey spotted Margot seated on the front deck, waiting for her. Zeke and Liam were in the water. Zeke was surfing, and eight-year-old Liam was body-boarding. In a few hours, all of them would be going to the park together.

Margot waved, and Bailey parked and joined her on the deck. Bailey's dad used to be Margot's agent. At one time, Margot had been a child actor on a prime-time sitcom. Years later, she'd starred in a sequel to the old show. These days, she was delving into film.

"Morning," Margot said, her wavy red hair blowing in the breeze. "Do you want a cup of coffee?" She gestured to the carafe. "Or would you rather have orange juice?" That was on the table, too, along with toasted bagels.

"I'll do the OJ." Bailey took a chair and poured herself a glass. She went for a bagel, too, slathering it with cream cheese. "How was New York?" Margot had been in Manhattan, meeting with a director about his latest film.

"It went well. My part is small, but it's really pivotal to the plot. I'm excited about it." Margot leaned forward in her seat. "How was the first night of the reunion? I'm sorry I missed it. I hated leaving you all alone."

"I wasn't alone. I spent the evening with Wade Butler. We ate together, we talked, we danced." Just thinking about him made her pulse spike. "We even confronted Shayla Lewis. I'm going to be sending her information about my foundation."

"Wow. Sounds like you had interesting night. Is Wade going to make a donation?"

"Yes, and we're supposed to talk more about it today. He offered to help bring in other sponsors, too." She tasted her bagel, then waited a beat before she said, "He's just the sexiest guy. Like, so damn hot now. I even thought about taking him home with me." She grabbed a napkin and crumpled it. "But you know how careful I am about getting involved with anyone. He says he's cautious, too. But that still doesn't mean we should hook up."

Margot gazed out at the ocean, where Zeke and Liam were playing in the waves. "I wish you weren't so skittish about meeting the right man."

"You've been skittish, too. You've been through hell and back with my brother." Bailey sighed. "I think I'm better off alone. I get the feeling Wade is, too. He agreed with me that love seems more painful than it's worth."

Margot cocked her head. "You had a conversation about love?"

"Yes, but mostly we discussed sex. I kept bringing it up without meaning to." She still felt the effect of being near him. "He just made me so…hungry." A craving she couldn't seem to shake.

"Your brother has always affected me that way, too. You know how hard I worked to get Zeke out of my blood."

"And now you're going to walk down the aisle with him again." Bailey couldn't imagine what that would be like. She wasn't marriage-minded. She'd never even gotten the concept of playing house when she was little.

"Did Wade mention his prison stint?" Margot asked, drawing her back into the moment.

"We talked a little bit about it. But there's so much about him that I don't know. That I'll probably never know. He definitely has a mysterious side."

"I remember what a loner he was in high school. But you and I had our problems back then, too."

Bailey nodded. Margot had been bullied, too. Prior to high school, she'd been tutored on the set of her first sitcom, and by the time she'd attended Bev West, she'd become a teenage has-been from a canceled show the other kids poked fun at. But she'd grown out of that, blossoming into the person she was today. "You're doing great now. You're the happiest I've ever seen you."

Margot reached over to touch her hand. "I want you to be happy, too."

"Don't worry about me. I love my work, my house, my solitude. I have a lot to be thankful for. I just don't know if being happy with a man is possible."

And for now, Bailey wasn't even going to try.

By the time Wade arrived at the park, Bailey had already sent him a text, letting him know that she was there, too, on a grassy knoll near the merry-go-round.

He could see the carousel in the distance, but he hadn't answered her yet. For now, he was getting the lay of the entire land. He spotted Shayla and her crowd smack-dab in the middle of everything. She noticed him, as well, but quickly looked away. Was he making her uncomfortable? He hoped so.

Shutting Shayla out of his mind, he texted Bailey. She responded, asking if he wanted to meet at the merry-go-round. He replied with a thumbs-up and headed in that direction. But even so, he wasn't as upbeat as his text implied. It was Family Day at the reunion, a reminder, at least for him, that he didn't have a family anymore.

He approached the fence that surrounded the merry-go-round and caught sight of Bailey. She sported a blue top, paired with cutoff shorts and bright white sneakers. Her hair wasn't loose. She'd plaited it into a single braid. Wade's casual attire included sunglasses. His current mood required shielding his eyes.

"Hi," Bailey said when they came face-to-face.

"Hi, yourself." He itched to touch her hair, to unbraid it. Just as he'd longed to undo her twisty bun last night. Damn, but she drove him mad. "Most of the reunion folk are out that way." He gestured to the area where he'd come from. "Not that I care. But I'm pointing it out, in case you want to move closer to the masses."

"I'm actually good with being over here. It's private, but still close enough to see what's going on and get involved if we want to. Besides, I have nice memories of the merry-go-round. My dad used to bring me here to ride it when I was little."

Wade glanced at the carousel. Lots of kids were riding it now, the horses moving up and down, the organ music playing. "I've never been on it. I didn't come to this park when I was little."

"We should ride it later with Liam. I can't wait for you to meet him. He's playing Frisbee with my brother right now." She added, "Zeke is my half brother. He's five years older than me, and we have different dads. His was Samoan and Choctaw, and mine was white, obviously. We don't look anything alike, but you probably already saw pictures of him and Margot on my Instagram."

Wade nodded. He'd learned that her brother was a bodyguard who owned a personal protection company. "Did Zeke go to Bev West or did your parents send him somewhere else?" She'd never said much about him when they were younger.

"He went there. He was away in college by the time I was enrolled, so no one ever made much of a connection between us. He liked high school, though. It wasn't a problem for him." She frowned. "But he was still miserable being the son of a celebrity. He struggled with the paparazzi and gossip rags and all of that. I hated that side of it, too."

"I wouldn't know." And he hoped that he never

had to find out. He suspected that if anyone ever un-
covered his family history, the press would jump all
over it, especially with that damned newsmagazine
show that had laid out his dad's crimes. But luckily
the show hadn't made a connection to Wade. No one
knew who his father was. That was a secret his mom
had kept, even from Wade. He hadn't discovered the
truth until after she died.

"Shall we go?" Bailey asked and led him over to
her family. Or to Margot, anyway. At the moment,
she was the only one around, occupying a plaid blanket.

Margot stood to greet him. She still looked like
the same feisty redhead she'd always been, even if
she'd matured into a well-respected actress. At Bev
West, they'd only become friends because of their
mutual association with Bailey. But for Wade, just
about everything centered around Bailey back then.

"It's so nice to see you," Margot said, reaching out
to embrace him. "You're quite the success today."

"So are you." He glanced past her and spotted
Zeke heading toward them with Liam in tow. The
boy tromped along, carrying a Frisbee, and the man
was as big as a mountain, walking tall and straight
and with plenty of purpose.

"Am I about to get my ass kicked?" Wade asked
Margot. Zeke looked even tougher in person than in
his pictures. "That fiancé of yours might not appreciate this little hug of ours."

She laughed and released Wade from her clutches.

"Oh, don't mind him. I'm sure he'll cut you some slack."

"I hope so." Wade was only kidding, but he still wouldn't want to get on the other man's bad side.

Zeke scooped Liam up and carried him the rest of the way. When he reached Wade, he stopped in front of him and said, "You must be Bailey's old high school buddy." He introduced himself and shook hands, extending the arm that wasn't holding the kid. He introduced Liam next. The boy grinned and shook hands, as well. He did everything Zeke did. He was cute as hell, with blondish-brown hair and innocent brown eyes.

Everyone settled onto the blanket, drinking the flavored water Margot had packed in a cooler.

Liam chatted incessantly, excited about the games the committee had arranged. But first the caterers would be serving lunch. The scent of barbecue spiced the air.

About fifteen minutes later, they hit the chow line and returned to the blanket to eat. Wade learned all sorts of information from Liam. Along with the upcoming wedding, Zeke was in the process of adopting the boy. But Liam didn't want to start calling him "Dad" until it was finalized, because he hadn't called Margot "Mom" until she'd officially adopted him.

Liam was excited about everything, including Bailey becoming his aunt. He spoke adoringly about her and prattled about a children's book that he and Bailey had written together. The proceeds were going to a foster care charity. Liam had been a foster kid before Margot had come into his life.

As Wade listened to Liam sing his new family's praises, he thought about the creative writing class he'd had with Bailey during their freshman year. In fact, it was the first time he'd ever seen her. He'd loomed in the back of room, and she'd sat up front, perched diligently in her chair. He used to watch her, fascinated by how talented she was. The teacher had always read her stories out loud. Wade had gotten high marks on his, too, but he was nowhere near the writer Bailey was.

"Are you enjoying your food?" she asked him.

He turned to face her. "Yeah. It's good." Balancing his plate on his lap, he removed his sunglasses and hooked them onto the front of his T-shirt, wanting to get a better look at her. "Are you going to play any of the games with Liam?"

"Oh, for sure." Her pretty blue eyes lit up. "We're both going to do the gunny sack race. It's supposed to be the first one, and it's for all ages."

Wade broke into a smile, impressed with her enthusiasm. "I'll stand off to the side and cheer you on."

Liam overheard their conversation and said, "They're giving away first- and second-place prizes. Maybe me and Bailey will win. Then she can give me both prizes."

"Oh, really?" She shot him a competitive look. "What makes you think I'm going to give away my prize?"

Liam laughed, but Wade suspected that she would give the kid anything he wanted. They shared a closeness that couldn't be denied. Wade had never bonded with anyone, aside from his fragile-hearted mom, and she'd been gone a long time. He just wished that she hadn't been so tight-lipped about his father. That still hurt, deep in the pit of his soul.

When the start of the games was announced, Bailey and Liam leaped up to play, and Wade tagged along for support.

It was fun to watch, but neither Bailey nor Liam came anywhere near winning. Liam gave it his all, hopping along like a rabbit, but he was just too slow. Bailey tripped and stumbled a few times, wobbling to get back on her feet. Wade wanted to dash out there and help her up, but she didn't need him coming to her rescue. She was a grown woman running a silly race, not a teenager being bullied at school.

The picnic continued, offering more games and activities. Ice cream was served, too. Wade went for two scoops of mint chocolate chip. Bailey outdid him with three scoops, combining strawberry, rocky road and cookies and cream. She got full and pawned some of the strawberry off on him. It made him think about the mushrooms from last night. He took her ice cream willingly, eating straight from her cone.

He caught Zeke and Margot watching them, and Wade realized how openly flirtatious he and Bailey were being. But it was just a way to blow off some steam. Or he hoped it was. He didn't want to go home immersed in sinful thoughts of her.

After everyone finished their ice cream, Bailey suggested that she and Wade take Liam on the merry-go-round. The kid was definitely up for it, grabbing Bailey's hand as they walked toward the carousel. Wade wanted to hold her hand, too, but he refrained, trying to keep his attraction to her at bay.

After they bought their tickets and waited in line, she said, "Walt Disney used to take his daughters here to ride this very same merry-go-round. But you know the best part? It was on one of those outings that he got the idea to create a place where families could gather and have fun." She bumped Liam's shoulder. "And that idea became Disneyland."

"I love Disneyland!" the boy exclaimed.

"Me, too," Bailey replied. "And it's cool to know that this merry-go-round helped inspire it."

"Did your dad tell you that story when he used to bring you here?" Wade asked her.

She nodded. "He told me about how many times it's been used in films and TV shows, too. Did you know my dad was a talent agent?"

"You mentioned it briefly when we were young." But nonetheless, it was clear that Bailey had been close to her father. As endearing as it was, Wade couldn't relate. He'd screwed up with Carl, a hardworking guy who'd tried to be a good stepfather to him, but he couldn't go back and fix it. Carl had died while Wade was in prison. As for his real dad, he was just a slick, handsome con man who broke women's hearts, leaving Wade with a bloodline that felt horribly tainted.

After the carousel ride, Wade reached for his sunglasses, intending to put them back on, when he discovered that they were no longer hooked to his shirt. Had they slipped off on the merry-go-round? Or had he lost them earlier? He sure as hell wasn't going to retrace his steps to find them. He had plenty of other pairs at home. Besides, he had to head out soon. He remarked that it was nearly time for him to go, and that he and Bailey still needed to discuss her charity.

"Then we better hurry things along," she said.

He agreed, and once he said goodbye to her family, he and Bailey went for a walk. At this point, her braid was a little messy and so were her clothes. Plus, her cheeks were pink from the sun. He suspected that her skin would be warm to the touch.

Finally, they stopped walking and sat beneath a shady tree. He glanced toward the reunion. The other guests seemed far away now. He and Bailey were alone.

"Will you send me a copy of your business plan?" he asked. "I'll need more information before I can pitch it to my friends and associates."

"Yes, of course. I'll do it right away. Just text me your email address and I'll attach it." She smiled. "Your help means the world to me."

"I'm glad to do it." Her cause felt like his cause, too. An experience they'd shared when they were young. "What's your biggest expense? What aspect should I be pitching the hardest?"

"Definitely the education center. As soon as I have the funds, I'm going to start scouting a location for it. I want it to have a homey feel, a place where we can raise awareness and host fund-raisers for our events. I'd like to host fund-raisers for other anti-bullying organizations, too. There's so many good programs out there that need attention."

"That sounds amazing." He made a sardonic joke. "Maybe Shayla can be one of your keynote speakers."

Bailey laughed. "Her and Randall Kincaid. I'll just run right out and get on that."

He laughed a little, too. Then he said, "As soon as you send me your information, I'll make a sizable contribution." He hadn't decided on the amount yet, but he wanted her to know it would be substantial.

"Thank you." She pressed a hand to her chest. "That's so generous of you. I'm humbled to have you in my corner."

Wade was equally humbled by her. She made him want to be a better person. But she'd always made him feel that way, or he wouldn't have swooped in to protect her in high school.

He checked the time on his phone. "I need to go, but maybe we can video chat in a few weeks and see where I'm at with acquiring other donors. Or I can come back to LA and we can meet up in person."

He had the unsettling urge to return, to be physically near her again. "I can book a room at the same hotel."

She went silent before she said, "Another option is for you to be my houseguest." She quickly clarified, "I have an extra bedroom where you can sleep, and you staying with me would give us more time to hang out and work together."

He hesitated, uncertain if he should accept. But he couldn't seem to say no. He wanted to be in her company, even if being under the same roof seemed risky. "Thank you. I'd like to be your houseguest."

"Then it's a date." She fumbled. "Well, not a date, exactly. But you know what I mean." She smoothed her hair, struggling to tame the wispy strands coming loose from her braid. "Just let me know when you'll be available."

"It'll probably be the weekend after next, but I'll check my schedule. For now, I better get to the airport before my pilot thinks I went AWOL." He stood and dusted off his jeans.

She climbed to her feet, as well, and they stared at each other. She broke eye contact first, and he released a shuddered breath.

"I'll be in touch," he said. He had no idea what sort of trouble he was headed for, but damn if he wasn't going to find out. Seeing Bailey again was just too tempting to resist.

Four

Bailey had spent the past two weeks revising a script, but now she was free from work and dashing around her house, getting ready for Wade's visit. She kept reorganizing and trying to make everything look presentable. Which was foolish, she thought, because her place was already organized, just not in a conventional way.

She collected books, flowerpots, old teakettles and vintage typewriters. Her homemade crafts included wall hangings, refrigerator magnets and candles. She also concocted lotions, shampoos, body washes and lip balms. Her backyard flourished with vegetables, herbs and fruit trees, all of which she tended herself. She wasn't interested in hiring a gardener, housekeeper or chef. She'd grown up in a sprawling mansion, where everything had been done for her, and she'd hated it. For Bailey, cutting her own grass, cleaning her own house and cooking her own meals was a joy.

Her three-bedroom, two-bath hideaway was positioned at the top of a winding road, surrounded by oaks, willows and sycamores. Groves of evergreen decorated the land, too. Chaparral grew in abundance.

She entered the guest room where Wade would be staying. She'd remade the bed three times. But mostly she kept touching it because she couldn't quit thinking about him sleeping there.

Did he sleep naked? Was he an early riser? Did he take long, hot showers? Would he use the shampoo and body wash she'd made for him?

Bailey opened the blinds a bit more, letting the sun in. Wade was due to arrive within the hour. Had she made a mistake, inviting him to stay at her home?

Maybe, but she couldn't seem to stop herself. She wanted to spend as much time with him as possible.

She sat on the edge of the bed and ran her hand across the bedspread. Wade lived a much more upscale life than she did, relying on the trappings his wealth provided. But he hadn't been a rich kid. His upbringing had been different from hers. Nonetheless, they'd both been bullied, and that was why they'd be working together on her foundation. She appreciated everything he was doing to boost her non-profit. He'd become her greatest Free Your Heart ally.

She stood and smoothed the spot on the bedspread where she'd been sitting. She'd almost slept in this bed last night, just to curl up on the same mattress where he would soon be. But she'd changed her mind, worried that it made her seem a little stalker-ish. She'd never had this kind of sexual obsession over anyone else before.

She used to reprimand Margot about her obsession with Zeke, and now Bailey was lusting after Wade. But that didn't mean she was going to have an illicit affair with him. Their relationship was strictly busi-ness. Or that was what she kept telling herself. At this point, she feared that she might jump him the minute he appeared at her door.

No, no. Bailey shook her head. She knew better than that.

She exited the guest room and went into the kitchen to make a pitcher of lemonade, determined to stay strong.

The lemons were from one of her trees. She had no idea if Wade even liked lemonade, but the fridge was stocked with other beverages, too. And food. She intended to cook for him this weekend. It was the least she could do, considering how generous he was being with his time and money.

She finished making the lemonade, then realized that she'd spent more energy on preparing her house for Wade's visit than she had on her appearance. She wasn't wearing a speck of makeup, and her hair hung down her back in a haphazard ponytail.

How typical of her. She rushed into her bathroom to make herself more presentable. She added a bit of color to her face and worked her hair into fishtail ponytail, making it a little cuter than it was before.

She checked out her clothes in the mirror. She wore a 1970s halter top and a pair of slightly torn jeans. She liked her outfit, even if she looked like a throwback from the counterculture era. But what the heck. Laurel Canyon used to be the nucleus of folk and rock hippiedom. Besides, Bailey wasn't a fashionista like her mother. She didn't have a personal stylist who picked out her wardrobe. She preferred garage sales, flea markets and Monday afternoons at the Goodwill. Her rebellion, she supposed, for never quite fitting into the Beverly Hills mode. Even the trendy little dress she'd worn to the reunion had come from a thrift store.

She gazed at her reflection, wondering what sort of women Wade dated. He'd made it clear that he was cautious about his lovers, but he'd never specified a type. Whatever the case, he was definitely attracted to her, just as she was to him.

When the doorbell rang, Bailey turned away from the mirror so fast, she nearly bumped into the bathroom door.

Was that Wade? Was he here already?

She took a deep breath, warning herself to relax.

But then she ran down the hall anyway, rife with nerves.

Mindful of her privacy, she peered out the peephole to make sure it was him. Yes, indeed. There he was. Her old schoolboy crush turned ex-con turned billionaire.

Bailey opened the door, and Wade said, "Hello" in a glad-to-see-you voice, making her pulse jump and jive.

She invited him inside, and as soon as he crossed the threshold, he roamed his gaze over her, making her instantly aware that she wasn't wearing a bra. So much for her halter top. She should've made a less bohemian choice. Her damned nipples were poking through the fabric. Her only consolation was that the busy print acted as camouflage. Still, she was aroused underneath, affected by his presence.

He looked gorgeous, with his hair swept away from his forehead and a backpack slung over his shoulders. Today his eyes were green with just a touch of gray.

"Let me show you around," she said, taking him to the guest room first. "This is where you'll be staying."

"Thank you." He placed his backpack on the bed—the bed she'd been preoccupied with earlier—and walked over to the window. "It has a great view of the canyon." He turned back to face her. "It's really secluded."

She gestured to his bathroom. "I made you some

shampoo and body wash. But you don't have to use them."

"You *made* them? Then I'll use them for sure." He went into the bathroom to check out her potions.

She stood back while he opened the bottles and sniffed them. Finally, she inched closer, joining him.

She said, "For the body wash, I added a bit of cedarwood oil to give it a masculine scent. The shampoo has peppermint and tea tree oil."

"I appreciate you thinking of me. It's kind of sexy, too, knowing I'll be showering with stuff you made." He capped the bottles. "Sorry, I shouldn't have said that."

"It's okay." She fidgeted with the hem of her top, still wishing she'd hadn't gone braless. "I should finish showing you around."

He nodded, and she walked him from room to room, skipping her bedroom and en suite bathroom. She figured she should leave that off the tour. There was no reason for him to see where she slept and bathed and fantasized about him.

"This house used to be a hunting cabin," she said as they entered her office. "It was built in the 1920s, but it's been remodeled since then."

"It's charming. It suits you, Bailey." He wandered over to the shelves where she kept her typewriter collection. "These are cool. There's such a mystique about old machinery and technology."

"I think so, too." She glanced at the tattoo on his wrist. She remembered him telling her in high school, when he'd first gotten it, that the symbols were early computer code. "Would you like some lemonade? It's fresh squeezed."

He turned away from the typewriters. "That sounds good." He moved closer to where she stood. "Is the lemonade homemade? Another one of your talents?"

"I like to keep busy." For now, her mind was busy, cluttered with thoughts of him.

She invited him to sit on the patio while she served the lemonade. The mountain air was crisp and clean, and as she joined him at the glass-topped table, he glanced around her yard. She noticed how observant he was, taking everything in.

"It's all so pretty," he said.

She assumed he meant the landscape. But then she wondered if his comment was meant to include her. That he was also saying how pretty she was, in her colorful clothes—with her nipples poking out like cherry pits.

"It's a nice day, too," he added.

Bailey only nodded. A small breeze had kicked up, pulling her top tighter against her body. "What did you think of my business plan?" she asked, pushing past the small talk. He was looking at her with far too much fascination in his eyes.

He blinked and responded, "It was excellent. In fact, I've got quite a few pledges and donations lined up for you. But the biggest score was a piece of property in Pasadena. It's a Victorian-era house that an associate of mine has been lending to nonprofits for their fund-raisers. But now he'd like to donate it to your foundation so you can use it as your education center. It's commercially zoned and would be a great location for you." Wade leaned forward in his chair. "There's a catch, though."

Bailey suspected there would be. Lots of donors and sponsors had stipulations. "What does he want?"

"He's a real estate magnate, an older gentleman who owns properties all over the world, but he loves hobnobbing with the Hollywood crowd. He wants your foundation to host a black-tie fund-raiser there. And he wants a guarantee that your mother will attend. He's dying to meet her."

She gripped her glass. "You told him I was Eva Mitchell's daughter?"

"No. He researched you on his own. But it's just one fund-raiser. One fancy gala, then the place will officially be yours."

It sounded so simple. But to Bailey, it was complicated. "That's a wonderful offer, and I hope I don't seem ungrateful. But I'm not comfortable involving my mother. She knows that I was bullied when I was young, but she has no idea that it revolved around me being her daughter or the extent that I suffered because of it. I never worked up the nerve to tell her the entire story. But if she's the string that ties me to the property, I'd feel like a fraud keeping the truth from her."

Wade gently replied, "If the stakes are too high,

you don't have to accept the property. I can decline for you."

"Maybe I just need more time to think about it. I mean, if I keep hiding the details from my mom, how am I supposed to tell my story publicly, too?"

"You don't have to tell everyone everything, Bailey."

"I know." She'd intended to keep the most humiliating parts to herself. "But is it hypocritical of me to launch an antibullying campaign and gloss over my own experiences?"

He glanced away, and she wondered if he was keeping shameful secrets, too. But she had no right to pry. She had enough issues of her own.

She heaved a sigh. "Regardless of what I decide, I'm impressed with your efforts. You've managed to do more in these past two weeks than the months I spent trying to get everything off the ground."

He shrugged. "I have lots of connections."

"I do, too. But in my case, most of the A-listers I know are associated with my family, and I try to steer clear of that. Even as a screenwriter, I did my best to forge an independent path." She leaned forward. "I'm not saying that I haven't benefited from having successful parents. My dad left me more than just his truck. I bought this house with my inheritance. It's my haven. A place for me to hide out when I need to immerse myself in my work."

"It's definitely a great spot for that, but it's nice that you haven't fenced it in. I like how open it is."

"Thanks. Keeping it open is important to me. The biggest threat to the wildlife in this area is fencing things in. But I'm not completely without barriers. I have garden fences." Rustic wood enclosures that she'd built herself. "I'd never fence the borders, though. I want the wildlife to be able to roam free. I like hearing the coyotes howl at night."

"Then I guess I'm going to hear them while I'm staying with you, too."

Yes, she thought. He would be in the room next to hers, hearing what she heard. "Are you a light sleeper?"

He nodded. "I've always been that way."

"Me, too." Would they lie awake at the same time, thinking about each other, struggling through their attraction?

"Why do coyotes howl so much at night?" His voice turned rough. "It's not a mating ritual, is it?"

Her skin went warm, the late-afternoon sun shining down on them. "They do have an invitation howl that's associated with mating. But mostly they howl to communicate and avoid territorial conflicts."

"I figured you'd know what their deal was."

"I like to research things." She noticed his lemonade was nearly gone. "Do you want a refill?" she asked.

"No, thanks. But I was thinking that I could take you to dinner. Maybe an early meal?"

"If you don't mind, I'd rather cook. It's my way of thanking you for all your help."

"Then who am I to refuse? I'll take whatever you give me." He gazed breathlessly at her. "Anything at all."

Her pulse jumped. "Are you hungry now? Should I get started on it?"

"I definitely am," he replied.

So was Bailey. Only her hunger went beyond food. Apparently his did, too. But dinner was all they were going to have.

While Bailey worked in the kitchen, Wade went into his room and unpacked his belongings. Mostly he just needed a minute to quell the heat of wanting her. He considered taking a quick shower just so he could use the body wash she'd made. But that would only fuel his fire. This wasn't the time to strip off his clothes and douse himself in the scent she'd chosen for him. That seemed too animalistic, somehow. Too primal.

He just needed to get his desire in check. He finished emptying his backpack and headed to the kitchen.

Bailey stood at the stove, cooking up a storm. She'd put a full-size apron over her clothes, but her back was still exposed. The strings on the apron did little to hide the bareness of her skin.

"Can I assist you?" he asked her.

She spun around, obviously unaware that he'd been hovering in the doorway. "Oh my goodness. You scared me."

"Sorry." He glanced at the front of her apron. He'd noticed her pert little nipples earlier, but he couldn't see the outline of them now. "I was offering my help."

"Oh, okay." She gestured to the counter. "You can slice the cucumbers for the salad."

"Will do. What are you making, exactly?"

"Chicken scallopine with lemon-butter pasta, sautéed spinach and oven-roasted asparagus. The salad is a cucumber and strawberry recipe with poppy seed dressing."

"Damn. Where did you learn to cook like this?"

"I used to follow our chef around when I was a kid. I followed everyone around. The landscapers, the maintenance staff, the housekeepers. I wanted to know how to do everything they did."

She moved like lightning, getting the meal done while he worked on the cucumbers. He managed to clean and slice the strawberries, too, so he wasn't completely useless. The poppy seed dressing was already mixed.

They ate at the dining room table, surrounded by her shabby-chic furniture and eclectic knickknacks. To him, it looked like beautiful chaos, with every nook and cranny filled. He wondered if she would be as unconventional in bed, tumbling him and the sheets. Not that he was supposed to find out. She hadn't invited him here for an affair.

He complimented her on the dinner. It was truly delicious. Her apron was gone now, but she'd put a sweater over her top, claiming the air-conditioning in the house always made her a little chilly. He suspected that she was just trying to cover up.

"Have you been to the property in Pasadena?" she asked suddenly. "Have you seen it?"

"No. But all I have to do is call the caretakers and they'll show it to us, if you decide that you're interested." He paused. "I'm sorry it comes with strings attached."

"And I'm sorry I'm being so sensitive about my mom, but my relationship with her has always been difficult." Bailey twined some noodles around her fork. "It's wild that your associate is willing to give away a piece of property just to have the opportunity to meet her."

"I'm sure he's hoping to dance with her, too."

"She does have that effect on men. What's his name? You haven't mentioned it."

"It's Gordon Scott. He's in his eighties, so when I described him as older gentleman, I meant it."

"Oh, wow. I pictured a guy around my mom's age. She's sixty-two." Bailey winced. "As charmed as her life has been, she's suffered some tragedies. She's been widowed twice."

Wade's curiosity was piqued. "Is that why you think loves hurts?"

"That's part of it. But the way my dad doted on my mom scared me, too. How desperate he always was to please her. I never wanted to feel what he was feeling for anyone. Then I got even more scared when Margot and Zeke fell in love and broke each other's hearts. They're happy now, but they used to be a mess." She glanced up from her plate. "What scared you away?"

He wasn't about to tell her what his dad had done to his mom in the supposed name of love, but he couldn't avoid her question, either. He owed her at least a partial explanation.

He said, "After everything I've been through, I just don't have it in me to get close to anyone. I worked hard to get back on my feet after prison, but it still made me more of a loner than I already was." Explaining further, he added, "I have some nice friends, but it's not like you are with Margot." He didn't have anyone that special. "As for my lovers, I prefer to keep a bit of distance. I've never even done the friends-with-benefits thing. They've either been my lover or my friend."

"They can't be both?"

"I don't know. I've never tried it." He compartmentalized his life to the best of his ability. "I haven't had a lover in a while, though. I don't need someone all the time."

"I'm not as alone as you are. Like you said, I have Margot. But I can relate to how you feel about your lovers. I've never gotten overly close to any of mine, either, and it's been a while since I've been with anyone."

He didn't respond, and they both went silent, finishing the meal she'd made. He gazed across the table at her, wishing he could seduce her into his bed. Or climb into hers. Whatever the case, he just wanted to feel her body next to his. His needs might be sporadic, but at the moment, he had a powerful need for her. A hankering he'd had since high school. There wasn't another woman on earth he could say that about.

After dinner, he helped her clear the table, and they spent the rest of evening streaming an old movie and stealing sultry glances at each other. She fussed with her sweater, tugging at the buttons, and he rubbed his sweaty palms on his jeans.

By the time they agreed to turn in, he was restless as hell and wanting her even more. But he said a proper good night and listened for the click of her door before he closed his and realized how alone he really was.

Wade couldn't sleep. He turned on the bedside lamp and reached for his phone, intending to scroll through the top news stories and entertain himself like every other insomniac, but instead, he climbed out of bed and got halfway dressed.

He went outside, following the sound of the coyotes. They'd been howling for what seemed like forever. He flipped a switch by the back door, illuminating the tiny string lights draped across the patio. The effect was magical. Just like Bailey, he thought.

He ventured toward her vegetable garden, walking barefoot on a stepping-stone path and still listening to the coyotes in the distance. Just as he stopped to glance up at the sky and marvel at how many stars there were, he heard the back door open.

He turned toward the noise and spotted Bailey on the patio, looking soft and shadowy in an oversize T-shirt that came to her knees, the pale fabric making her seem ghostlike.

"Wade?" she called out. "Is that you?"

"Yes, it's me." He headed in her direction and joined her on the patio. "What are you doing out here?"

"I always come outside when I can't sleep. But I didn't expect to see you. What were you doing prowling around?"

"I couldn't sleep, either. I got distracted by the coyotes. Then by the stars and now by you." He gentled his voice. "You look beautiful."

Her breathing hitched. "That's sweet of you to say, but you can barely see me."

"I can see you well enough with all these little string lights." Her hair was piled on top of her head and secured with two large clips, one on each side.

"They're called fairy lights. I put them up myself."

"You could be a fairy. All you need is wings." He tugged at the sleeve of her T-shirt. "Is this pink or white?" He couldn't tell. The lights weren't bright enough for that.

"It's lavender. But what about you? Aren't you cold without a shirt?"

"Not at all." He felt warmer than he should be. "But I'm dying to touch you right now."

"Oh, God, Wade. This is crazy. We're out here at night, just the two of us, when we should be alone in our beds."

"We didn't do it on purpose. It just happened this way."

"But I invited you to my house. I brought you here, and now I want you to touch me." She shivered, as if from the thought. "But if we go too far, there'll be no turning back."

"Let's just take it a step at a time." He removed the clips from her hair, set them on a nearby table and watched her mass of blond locks come tumbling down. "I've wanted to do this for so long." His fantasy was turning into a reality. "You're like Lady Godiva or Rapunzel or something. I'm so turned on right now."

"So am I." A heartbeat later, she asked, "Are you naked under your jeans?"

"Yeah." He grabbed a fistful of her hair, just to feel it flow through his fingers. "Are you bare under your shirt?"

"I have panties on. No bra, though."

He glanced down, catching a glimpse of her pebbled nipples. "You weren't wearing one earlier, but then you covered up with a sweater." He kept playing with her hair. Everything about her transfixed him. "What color are your panties?"

"They're the same shade as my skin."

Flesh-toned, he thought. His imagination soared, trying to envision her in them. "And what kind are they? What shape and style?" He longed to know every sensual detail.

"They're called boy shorts. Mine are smooth, no bows or lace or frills." She paused to catch her breath. "I feel like we're having phone sex, but without our phones."

"Maybe it's fairy-light sex." He realized that the coyotes were no longer howling. The canyon was quiet now. "Me with my fascination with your hair, and you with your boy shorts and imaginary wings."

"Are you going to kiss me?" she asked shakily.

"Are you going to let me?"

"Yes. I totally am." She leaned forward, encouraging him to take her mouth as deeply and passionately as he could.

Five

Bailey flung her arms around Wade's neck, bringing him closer, needing him, craving him. The kiss was hot and desperate, his tongue mating with hers, but that was how she wanted it.

The midnight air caressed her skin, yet a fire blazed through her body, through her pores. He backed her against a wall, and they both went a little mad. He lifted her up, and she wrapped her legs around his waist, the hem of her nightshirt bunching between them. They continued to kiss, over and over, hungry, eager.

Finally, when they came up for air, she huskily asked, "What step was that?"

He pressed his forehead to hers. He was still holding her off the ground, her legs wrapped around him. "What do you mean?"

"You said we were going to take this a step at a time." She could feel how incredibly hard he was beneath his jeans.

"It's the first one, I guess." He released a rough breath. "Or maybe the second. We might've skipped one somewhere."

She clung dizzily to him. "What are we supposed to do now?"

"That's up to you. If it was up to me, I'd kiss you all night."

"Just kiss?" She touched her lips softly to his. If they were naked, they'd be having sex by now. The position they were in would certainly work.

He held her tighter. "You're teasing me."

"I'm teasing myself, too." She was lost in the moment, steeped in the feel of him. "Come to my room with me, Wade." She wanted him, deep inside her.

He released her, and she put her feet back on the ground. "Are you sure? Because you're the one who said that if we go too far, there'll be no turning back."

"Yes, but we both know that we won't be lovers forever. That neither of us is the type to make a commitment. So maybe turning back doesn't matter." She skimmed a hand down his chest. "We can just be together for now." In her room, in her bed.

He covered her hand with his. "I hope you have protection. I didn't bring anything with me. I should have, considering how much I want you, but I didn't think we would actually—"

"I'm on birth control. I've been tested, too. I'm safe." She was a single woman. She didn't leave those sorts of things to chance.

He met her gaze. "I'm safe, too."

"Then let's do this." She led him to her bedroom. It was softly lit by the night-light she'd left on.

He said, "I should've known your room would look something like this."

She followed his line of sight. Her canopy bed was draped with mosquito netting, and her vanity table was littered with books instead of perfume bottles and cosmetics.

He stood back to study her. "Will you undress for me? Will you let me watch? I don't want to rush any of this."

There was no way she could refuse, not with the intensity in his eyes. "There isn't going to be much for me to remove."

"I still want to watch." He remained perfectly still.

She reached for the hem of her nightshirt. She wasn't skilled at the art of stripping, but Wade didn't seem to care what her process was, so long as it ended with her being bare.

She removed the shirt and stood before him in the underwear she'd told him about. Her breasts were exposed now, and he was checking out her pointy pink nipples.

After giving herself a moment to breathe, she

peeled off her panties and tossed them onto her reading chair.

He stared at her, and she tried not to feel self-conscious. She had a heart-shaped patch of pubic hair that she groomed herself. She hadn't mentioned that part to him, but now her quirky little secret was front and center.

She quickly clarified, "It's just something I do for my own amusement, not anyone else's."

He kept staring. "You really are one of a kind, Bailey. I've never known another woman like you."

He came forward and tugged her into his arms. She pressed herself against him, and he skimmed his hands down her spine, following each and every vertebra.

When he told her to lie down, she got into bed. He joined her, but he didn't remove his jeans.

Instead, he kissed her, then worked his way down her body, gliding his lips along her skin. She got goose bumps in every place he touched. This was her favorite kind of foreplay, even if it sometimes made her shy.

He hovered at the heart between her legs and parted her with his fingers. Bailey sucked in her breath, and he kissed her there, softly, slowly.

She meant to close her eyes, but she couldn't. She ached to see him. He looked so handsome in the scattered light, making love to her with his mouth. She touched his hair and realized how heavy hers was, strewn across her pillow, unbound for him.

He used his hands and his mouth, licking and kissing and rubbing. He glanced up at her, and she bit down on her bottom lip.

She clawed the bedding, making mewling sounds. The mosquito netting above her head looked hazier than it already was. She couldn't see straight anymore. She couldn't think clearly, either. Her long-ago crush, her brand-new lover, was making her come.

She shook and shivered, her body jolting against his mouth. She was warm and wet and sticky, and he reveled in it. He didn't stop until she cried out.

Grateful for the relief, she sank into the covers. He rose up to recline next to her, and she smiled at him. He smiled, too, right before he peeled off his jeans, reminding her that they weren't anywhere near finished.

Wade had never been so mesmerized, so aroused. He'd thought about Bailey so many times throughout the years, wondering how she was, hoping she was happy. And now she was naked in his arms, warm and wet from an orgasm he'd just given her.

"What's your favorite position?" he whispered against her ear. He wanted to please her in every way possible.

"It depends on who I'm with. But with you, I'd be willing to try anything." She slid her hand down, rubbing her thumb over the tip of his erection. "How do you want it?"

"I want it all." He felt like a kid in a candy store

that was on fire, trying to gather what he could before the flames devoured him. "But let's start here." He rolled onto his back and lifted her onto his lap.

She gazed down at him, her hair curtaining her face. She looked sweetly beautiful, with her perky breasts and valentine vagina. He reared up to kiss her, and the moment exploded.

She rubbed herself against him, letting him yearn for what came next. He wrapped his hands around her waist, getting ready for her to lift her hips, to take him inside.

She broke the kiss and leaned back, arching her body. Still circling her waist, he waited, desperate with need. She seemed content to tease him, a small smile tilting her lips.

Then she did it: she impaled herself.

Wade groaned from the pressure, and Bailey created a slow, slick rhythm, riding him like a cowgirl on a mechanical bull with the settings turned low. He helped her go up and down, guiding her, encouraging her to take him deeper. She leaned forward to kiss him, her hair spilling down over their bodies and tickling his chest.

After the kiss, she sat forward, maintaining the naughty rhythm. She touched herself, and he decided she was the most seductive lover he'd ever had.

"Look at you," he said. "Making yourself come." He wanted her to know how exciting this was for him, seeing her pleasure herself while she moved on his lap.

To Wade, it seemed strangely romantic, like the heart between her thighs. He could feel her pulse there.

Thumping. Thudding.

She closed her eyes and came in hot little ripples, giving him the satisfaction of watching her.

When she opened her eyes, he took control, changing positions and pinning her beneath him. He was on top now, setting the pace, taking what he needed. He pumped into her, thrusting from shaft to tip.

She moaned and wrapped her legs around him, slick and damp from her second climax. Would there be a third? He didn't know. All he wanted was to come himself.

They kissed like fiends, tongues sparring, teeth clashing. She clawed his back, and he lowered his head to suck on her nipples, one right after the other.

They rolled over the bed, their hands clasped and legs tangled. Frenzied as it was, he didn't lose his stride. He was still inside her.

Were the coyotes howling again or were the animalistic sounds just in his head?

He moved even harder and faster. Nothing mattered but the thrill of being with her, the primal heat and raw pleasure, the hammering of flesh against flesh. Sex, he thought. Rough, wild, hip-grinding sex. He could do this with her for a thousand years and never get enough. But that was his body talking. They'd be lucky if their affair lasted a few months.

She dug her nails into him again, and his appetite for her increased, making him wonder how that was even possible. He was already bone-deep in hunger. He remained braced above her, his stomach muscles bunching and quivering.

When she latched onto the sides of the canopy billowing over the bed, he hoped she didn't yank the filmy fabric down on top of them. At this point, anything seemed possible. She looked as reckless as he felt, pulling and tugging at anything that got in her way.

He shut out his thoughts and let his mind blur. His vision went wonky, too. He could barely see past the inferno shooting through his veins, every pinprick in his body centered at the spot where he and Bailey were joined.

Finally, he lost it, and the room began to spin, dragging him under into the depths of mayhem. He didn't care if an earthquake hit and the entire roof crashed down on them. Nothing could stop his climax now.

He came rough and quick, spilling into the woman panting beneath him. Holy hell, but it felt good. Wet and wild and rife with white-hot lust.

Before his arms gave out, he collapsed on top of her and buried his face in her hair, sweet silence settling between them.

Wade could've slept just how he was, nestled in Bailey's nakedness. But apparently she had other ideas.

She nudged at him and said, "I need to clean up. Do you want to take a bath with me?"

He lifted his head and peered down at her. "I do showers, not baths. Besides, how are we both going to fit in the tub? Unless the one in your bathroom is bigger than the one in the guest bath."

"It is. Much bigger. It's a cast-iron deep-soaking claw-foot with brass hardware. You'll be impressed."

"Why? Did you install it yourself?"

"No, smarty. It came with the remodel of the house. But I would've installed if I could've." She jabbed him in the ribs. "Now get off me and let me take my bath. Your weight is considerable for a waif like me."

He lifted his body from hers. "So now you're a waif? Last time you told me that I was supposed to refer to you as petite."

She sat up and swung her legs to the side of the bed. "Call me what you will, but you're still bigger and stronger than I am." She slanted him a sideways glance. "You've got some nice muscles on you. I like all of your parts, in fact."

"Oh, yeah?" Now he was tempted to give her a repeat performance, putting their parts together again. But she slipped out of bed and headed for the master bathroom.

As she retreated, all he saw was her hair, falling just short of her butt. She did have a cute little ass.

"Hold on!" he called after her.

She spun around. "Yes?"

"I'll give the bath a try. But the tub better be as impressive as you say it is." He climbed out of bed and followed her, enjoying the seductive game she was playing.

They entered the bathroom, and it was as charmingly cluttered as the rest of her house. The tub actually was pretty damn big. Or deep, at least. He would still have to bend his knees to sit in it. But not Bailey. She could stretch out all she wanted.

"I can't remember the last time I had a bath," he said. "I was a kid, for sure."

She rummaged through a drawer and produced some clips for her hair. She twined her locks into a bun and jammed the holders in place. "It was probably a bubble bath. Kids love those." She turned to face him. "We can add some to ours."

"Let me guess. You make your own bubbles?"

"Of course I do. And without the chemicals." She riffled through the amber bottles on a caddy beside the tub. "I have two recipes, one for relaxation and another for moisturizing the skin."

"Can we mix them together?" He watched her, amused by how serious she was about a bath.

"Yes, I suppose we could." She latched onto both bottles. "Then we'll be calm and moisturized."

"If you say so." He just liked being here with her. "I'll let you prepare it."

She went about the task, adjusting the temperature of the water and drizzling the homemade liquids under the spigot, creating a froth of white bubbles.

"You get in first, and I'll sit in front of you," she said.

"Yes, ma'am." He worked his way into the tub, almost expecting his bones to creak. But as the water surrounded him, he decided it wasn't half-bad.

She climbed in, and he made room for her, opening his legs so she could scoot in close. She wiggled her bottom, making herself comfy. She leaned back against him, and he slipped his arms around her.

She turned off the water when the tub was full and the bubbles were up to her chest. "You're the first man I've done this with. Baths are sort of sacred to me. Normally they're my alone time, but I wanted to share it with you."

He got the uncharacteristic urge to share his world with her, too. "Next time we get together, will you come to my house? I can have my pilot come get you."

"I'd love to see where you live." She tilted her head back to look at him. "But I can take a commercial flight. We used to fly on private jets when I was little, but it doesn't seem necessary to me now."

Most women were dazzled by his jet, but Bailey wasn't most women. She'd grown up in the lap of luxury. At this stage, though, Wade's net worth far exceeded her family's. Her mother was a millionaire, not a billionaire.

"You can travel however you want," he said. He nuzzled her hair, careful not to let the clips poke his face.

She reached for a washcloth and began sponging

herself off. When she washed between her legs, he nipped at her earlobe.

"You're wasting your time," he whispered. "I'm just going to come inside you again."

Her breath caught. Could she tell that she was making him hard? That he was nearly fully aroused?

"I've never done it in the bath," she said. "But I guess that stands to reason, since you're the first guy who's ever been in the tub with me."

He toyed with her nipples, rubbing his thumbs over them. "This would be a first for me, too, with my limited bath experience. I'm not even sure how to pull it off. But I'm willing to try."

She let go of the washcloth, and it disappeared into the bubbly abyss. "Maybe I can get on my knees to make it easier."

"I like that idea." He liked it a lot. "But I think we should drain the water first. Otherwise it might get sloshy or slippery."

"Better to be safe than sorry." She pulled the plug on the drain. She rinsed off with a handheld sprayer attached to the faucet.

Wade rinsed off, too, as she got down on all fours. He was beyond hard now. So damned aroused. She looked downright sinful in that position, offering herself to him.

He knelt behind her, and she gripped the front of the tub. He wrapped his arms around her waist, steadying her against him, and pushed inside. She keened out a moan and angled her hips to take him deeper. They were both probably going to be sore when this was over, cramped in a tub and abusing their bodies for the sake of sex. But it was worth every hot, hard, exciting minute.

They experimented together, finding their rhythm, moving back and forth. Wade decided that bathing with Bailey was fast becoming one of his favorite activities. He loved how pliable she was. How eager. How passionate.

He reached down to strum her, and she moaned under his onslaught. His sweet little fairy, he thought. He kept rubbing her, and she climaxed within no time, shuddering and making breathy sounds.

He was on the verge of coming, too, and he wanted nothing more than to spill into her. He looked down, watching himself thrust in and out.

He watched until his orgasm erupted, dragging him into a powerful surge of addictive pleasure and heart-quaking lust.

Bailey woke up in a state of confusion, with no sense of time or place. At least not until she squinted at the naked man sleeping next to her and everything came rushing back.

Wade. The object of her desire.

Was it possible to have a sex hangover? Because if it was, then that's what she had. After they'd messed around in the tub, they'd gone to bed and snuggled. But somewhere in the middle of the night, they'd awakened and gone after each other in the dark, without even saying a word. And now the sun was up, peeking into the room.

She leaned toward her nightstand, fumbled for her phone and glanced at the screen. It was high noon, but she wasn't headed to a gunfight. There was no hurry to get out of bed.

Still, she got up and padded across the floor for her robe. She removed it from its hook and slipped it on.

"Whatcha doin'?"

With a quick start, she turned in the direction of Wade's crackly voice. He lay on his side, tangled in her bedding, his hair flopped across his forehead, his eyes barely open. Was it obsessive that she wanted him again? That she imagined crawling back under the covers?

"I'm getting up," she replied, belting her robe and forcing herself to behave. These constant cravings couldn't be normal. She wasn't a cat in heat.

He pushed his fingers through his hair, brushing it away from his forehead. "What for?"

She sucked in her breath, wishing he didn't look so damned yummy. "To get coffee."

"Will you bring me a cup?"

"What flavor?" She intended to use the single-serve brewer instead of making a full pot. "I have a variety pack."

"It doesn't matter. Surprise me." A sleepy smile brightened his face. "I like surprises."

She seemed to recall him saying that he liked

women to bring him breakfast in bed, too. Should she fix food, as well? Or was coffee enough? She couldn't think past how badly she still wanted him.

"I'll be back." Anxious to escape, she darted out of the room.

The kitchen gave her an instant sense of peace, with its greenhouse window and wood-burning stove. She had a regular stove, too. But the antique one was her favorite, marking the vestiges of time. Sometimes Bailey wondered if she should've been born in another era, before the modern world took over. Which was especially weird now that she was sleeping with a guy who'd made his fortune in the tech industry. It didn't get any more modern than that.

She popped a French vanilla pod in the coffee machine for herself and chose hazelnut for Wade. Breakfast or lunch or whatever it would be at this hour would have to wait. Wade hadn't mentioned food, and for now, all she needed was coffee.

Bailey finished her task and returned to her lover. He was still naked, with a sheet draped over his waist. She handed him his cup. He thanked her, and she sat in her reading chair. She glanced down to see her underwear from last night, bunched up next to her on a needlepoint pillow. In a quick and seamless move, she pushed the panties under the pillow, hiding them for now. She didn't need any more reminders of the sexy things she'd been doing with Wade.

Were his eyes gray or green today? She couldn't

tell from this distance. They changed color depending on his mood or the lighting or the clothes he wore. Of course, at the moment, he wasn't wearing anything.

He sipped of his coffee. "This is good. Lots of flavor."

"I can't take credit. It comes that way." She tucked her hair behind her ears and wished she had pinned it up. Wade was looking at her as if she was a nymph who'd just come in from the garden. She shifted in her seat and asked, "Can we go see the Pasadena property today? I'm still debating what I should do about it."

"Sure. No problem. I'll call the caretakers and arrange it." He put his coffee down. "I like your robe, Bailey."

"Oh, thank you. It's from the 1940s." It was blush-pink silk with tiny yellow flowers, one of her favorites. "They used to call them dressing gowns. Sometimes I wear housecoats, too. But they're more grannnyish." She glanced at the pillow where her panties were hidden. "I like old clothes." She even had some vintage garter belts, but she wasn't going to mention those now.

He squinted. "Why are you sitting so far away from me? You're making me feel like the big bad wolf."

Her pulse jumped. "I'm just drinking my coffee. Mine is a vanilla roast."

"Can I try it? Will you come over here and give me a sip?"

Her limbs went weak. "Is that your ploy to get me back into bed?"

He fixed his gaze on her. "It could be. Are you going to take the bait?"

"You have no idea how hard I've been trying to keep my craving in check."

He raised his eyebrows. "For vanilla coffee?"

"For you, and you darned well know it. I came so many times yesterday you'd think I'd be out of orgasms by now." Yet it felt as if she could come just looking at him. "I've never been this way before."

"Me, neither. So that makes us even. Now get over here before we both explode."

Bailey left her chair in a whirl. She put her cup next to his, and he grabbed her, pulling her down and kissing her hard and quick.

He tugged at the belt on her robe, cursing when he couldn't open it fast enough. Once she was naked, he flung the garment over the side of the bed.

"There must be something wrong with us," she said as he pinned her beneath him and held her hands above her head. His eyes were gray and stormy.

"Whatever it is, let's just go for it." He stared down at her, as if he meant to eat her alive.

She tugged free from his hold and pulled him closer, wanting to devour him, too. He was her hunger, her obsession. A compulsion she feared she might never overcome.

Six

Bailey thought the estate in Pasadena was fabulous. For now, the caregivers were waiting outside, allowing her and Wade to look around by themselves.

The four-thousand-foot Queen Anne–style house boasted bay windows, peaked gables, a gorgeous stairwell and a wraparound porch. The backyard was landscaped with charming pathways and colorful gardens. The ballroom, which wasn't part of the original design but had been added on later, opened into one of the gardens.

Bailey turned toward Wade. "I can't believe Gordon is willing to donate this place to my charity. I love how beautifully it's been maintained."

"You could definitely use it as an education center. The ballroom could be set up for lectures. But it could still be used for fund-raisers and mixers. Plus, there are all sorts of other fund-raisers you could have, not just fancy balls, but picnics and outdoor activities, too."

"That's true. Only at first, I'd have to focus on the Hollywood fund-raiser Gordon wants me to host." The entire deal was contingent on that. But for Bailey, it also involved telling her mother the truth about why she'd been bullied. She took a deep breath, preparing to take the plunge. "I think I should accept Gordon's offer. I would be foolish to refuse it."

"I agree. You could definitely make use of this place."

Bailey nodded. "Everything about it will work, not just the ballroom and the yard, but this part, too." She glanced around the front parlor where they were standing. "This could be the reception area, and the back parlor could be used as office space." Overall, it was an amazing location. Gordon was even offering to pay for the caretakers to remain on the property. They lived upstairs, and from her understanding, they'd been invaluable when other charities had previously held functions here.

"When are you going to contact Gordon and let him know you're accepting his offer?" Wade asked.

"Not until I discuss it with my mom. She's going to have to agree to attend the fund-raiser he wants me to host."

"Do you think there's a chance she'll decline?"

"No. She loves parties, and I think she'll be flattered by Gordon's attention. But I'm going to be nervous talking to her about the things that happened to me in high school."

"When did you first tell her that you were bullied to begin with?"

"Honestly, I only just mentioned it this past spring, around the time I first started working on my foundation. I made it sound minor, compared to what it really was." Bailey released an audible breath, her anxiety mounting. She'd never been comfortable expressing her feelings to her mom. They'd just never been close. But some of that was her own fault; she'd chosen to keep the distance between them. "We rarely spend time together, and when we do, we tend to argue. I did stay with her for a few days after her most recent plastic surgery procedure, though. I offered to help her recover."

He lifted his eyebrows. "And how did that go?"

She laughed a little. "She drove me nuts, ordering me around and acting like a diva. But I'm still glad I did it. Even in spite of how bossy she was, I could tell that she appreciated having me there." Before Bailey's emotions ran away with her, she returned her attention to the house. "Should we finish checking things out?"

He nodded, and they took the stairwell to the bedrooms, where the caretakers lived. In the future, this area would be off-limits, but for today, it was part of the tour. Compared to the rest of the house, the bedrooms were small but no less charming, with old-fashioned wallpaper and modern furnishings.

"My house is a renovated Victorian, too," Wade said. "It still feels strange sometimes, living in a mansion and having so much space to myself. Especially for a guy who spent five years in a dormitory-style cell."

She couldn't imagine being in prison. But she knew what living in a mansion was like. "You went from one end of the spectrum to another. But I'll bet you have a great staff who look after your needs now." He'd mentioned some of them before.

He leaned toward her. "Yes, but it's not the same as having a fairy in my bed. I'll miss you when I go home."

"I'll miss you, too. But I'm far from being a fairy." Even if she secretly liked him referring to her that way. "I don't have magical powers."

"You do to me." He smiled, letting her know just what he thought those powers were.

She reached out to hold him, standing on her toes, stealing a quick kiss. They would miss each other for the sex. But now that they were lovers, would it get in the way of being friends? He'd never been friends with his lovers in the past, and now she wasn't certain of what to expect.

She stepped back and said, "I'm looking forward to visiting you, whenever we can arrange it."

"It's funny how we're eager to see each other again and I haven't even left yet."

"No, but you'll be leaving tomorrow." They had one last night together before he was gone.

Wade leaned on his elbow, gazing at Bailey. They were in bed, silent after a rowdy bout of sex.

"I'm hungry," she said, shattering the quiet.

He couldn't help but smile. "For food? Or is it me you want again?"

"Food." She sat up and grinned. "But no doubt I'll want you later."

"Likewise." He'd never known a woman with a more voracious appetite for him. He'd never wanted anyone as much as he wanted her, either. He couldn't wait until she visited him. He wanted to see her naked in *his* bed, sprawled out on *his* sheets and *his* pillows. But he wanted to wine and dine her, too, and show her his favorite parts of San Francisco.

Los Angeles was still painful for him. As much as he was enjoying his time with her, this city brought back too many disturbing memories, too much family crap. He had to give Bailey credit for fighting her family demons head-on. Wade preferred to bury his. No, that wasn't completely true. He'd done what he could to make good on his father's crimes and repair the lives his old man had destroyed. He'd handled that part, even if he'd done it secretly.

"Do you want a snack?" she asked. "I was thinking guacamole and chips."

"That sounds good. I'll help you make it." He didn't want to stay in bed, stressing about the bastard who'd spawned him. He couldn't work on that relationship the way Bailey could with her mom. Nor did he want to. Just the thought of his dad being released from prison someday made his skin crawl.

Wade knew that convicts could be reformed. He was one of them. But he didn't harbor that kind of hope for his father. At least his dad didn't know he existed. It wasn't as if his old man was going to come looking for him. That low-bellied snake had disappeared before Wade's mom even knew that she was pregnant. Plus, she'd never turned him in. The police didn't have a clue that she was one of his victims.

Still, Wade worried that someone might take an interest in his dad's case again. The show that had featured his other victims had originally aired four years ago, with little chance of reruns. But now the entire program was available on a streaming channel where anyone could watch it anytime. God forbid if his dad's episode picked up a huge audience or went viral, leaving the door open for amateur sleuths to uncover Wade's connection to it.

"Are you coming?" Bailey stood, peering down at him, already wearing her robe.

For a second, he merely blinked at her. He'd been so preoccupied that he hadn't realized that she'd gotten out of bed. Before she accused him of acting strange, he got up, put on his shorts and shot her a playful smile. "Fair warning, I like my guacamole hot."

"Me, too." She returned his smile. "The spicier the better."

They left the bedroom and entered the kitchen. She gathered the ingredients, placing everything on the counter.

He mashed the avocados, and she added red onion, fresh lime juice, sea salt, ground cumin, tomatoes and cilantro to the mix. Giving it the kick they both craved, she tossed in a serrano pepper instead of the traditional jalapeño.

"The seeds are what makes it hot," she said.

Wade nodded, eager to try it. It was her recipe, not his. He barely cooked. He'd only offered to help to free his mind.

Bailey removed a bag of tortilla chips from the pantry and dumped them into a big wooden bowl. "Now we eat."

He scooped some dip onto a chip and stuffed it into his mouth. If he hadn't been such a heat maven, steam probably would've been coming out of his ears. "Damn, that's good." He took another helping. "But now I want a margarita to go with it."

"Then let's make those, too. Do you like yours on the rocks, blended or straight up?"

"Blended, for sure." To him, it wouldn't be the same without the frozen slushiness.

"Me, too. But I just thought I'd check. Do you want to do the honors? Or should I?"

"I'll do it." He wasn't a cook, but he was a decent bartender. He went over to the bar in the living room and rounded up what he needed to make the margaritas from scratch. He didn't like using premade mixes.

After he prepared a pitcher, he salted the rims of their glasses and added fresh lime garnishes. Bailey gave him a thumbs-up, and they decided to eat and drink on the patio.

Wade sat across from her, anxious to arrange their next encounter. He asked, "What's your schedule like, in terms of you coming to visit me? I was thinking next weekend, if that works for you." He imagined rendezvousing with her every weekend, which was out of character for him. It would be okay, though, wouldn't it? He wasn't moving too fast, was he?

It was fine, he told himself. They were consenting adults, embarking on an affair. There was nothing wrong with that.

"Actually, that does work for me," she replied, her gaze locking onto his. "The only weekend I'm positively booked is the date of Margot and Zeke's wedding, and that isn't until October."

"I'm surprised you don't have any other plans between now and then. You seem pretty active to me."

"I guess it depends on how you define *active*. I attend writers' conferences when I can, but mostly I like to putter around in my garden on my days off. Or make lotions and potions. Or build tree houses."

"You don't have a tree house." Not that he'd seen. She did have a tree swing, though. He'd found that charming.

"I'm considering putting up a tree house. They have these really cute do-it-yourself kits. But I'd need some help with it. I don't think I could lift all that lumber by myself."

"I can help you." He made the offer before he could stop himself. He just kept making plans with her. "Or I could hire someone to do it for you."

"Now where'd be the fun in that?" She dipped into the guacamole and took a hearty bite.

"I'm going to spoil you when you're at my house. You're not cooking or cleaning or playing in the dirt."

"As if you could stop me." She tossed a chip at him.

He laughed and ate the chip. A second later, he said, "The offer still stands to use my jet, in case you change your mind about that."

"I don't know. Maybe I will. I am curious to meet your pilot and see if he dishes any secrets about you."

"No one knows my secrets." No one at all. "But there's not much to tell, anyway," he added, trying to seem as if he wasn't hiding anything that mattered. "Just the usual evil billionaire stuff," he joked.

She slanted him a sideways glance. "You have a solid reputation. Except for being an ex-con. But no one is holding that against you anymore."

"I'm an upstanding citizen now." Something he'd strived to be. But he still hated that he'd been conceived in such a lying, cheating way. He still ached for his long-lost mother, too, and the heartbreak she'd endured.

He hoped that no one ever broke Bailey's heart. She'd already been through enough turmoil when they were young. Sweet, sensitive Bailey, with her fragile wings. He'd protected her in high school, but he couldn't protect her forever.

Damn, he thought. What if he was the one who ended up hurting her? What if they got closer than they should, creating problems later on? He definitely needed to be mindful of how things unfolded between them. But for now, he was immersed in being her lover, as well as her friend.

"Why are you staring at me like that?" she asked.

"Like what?" he responded, feigning confusion.

"Like you're worried about me. You're not concerned that I'm biting off more than I can chew with my foundation, are you?"

"Not at all. I wouldn't be helping you with it if I didn't think you were capable of making it a success." He swigged his margarita and nearly gave himself brain freeze. "You're mistaken about the way I was looking at you. I'm not worried about anything." Or anything he was willing to admit. Wade was keeping his mixed-up feelings to himself.

Bailey curled up in bed with Wade, wishing she wasn't feeling so clingy about him leaving this morning. She'd already agreed to visit him next week, yet, somehow, that seemed like an eternity. She needed to get a grip on her attachment to him. But at least she wasn't the dreamy type, desperate to find love. She was immune to that, and so was Wade.

It was nice, though, reclining in his arms with

her head on his chest, listening to the steady beat of his heart.

"Are we still friends?" she asked him.

He nuzzled the top of her head with his chin. "Yes, of course we are. Why would you even ask me something like that?"

"Because you said that you've never been friends with any of your other lovers before, so I thought maybe you'd want to keep things separate."

"It's different with you. We were already friends when we were young. We didn't just show up in each other's lives. We have a history."

"A history of being bullied." A pain they would always share. "I'm going to go see my mom later today and talk to her about everything."

"Did your dad know what was going on? Is it something you ever discussed with him?"

Her memories rushed to the forefront. "I wanted to when it first started happening, but he was so absorbed with Mom and her crisis at the time, I kept quiet. She was in her forties then and panicking about maintaining her sex-symbol status. Dad was jumping through hoops to keep her insecurities in check, and I didn't want to stress him out even more. He was concerned about my stuttering, but it was much more prevalent at school than it was at home, so my family never really saw it at its worst." Bailey let out the breath she was holding. "Dad still made sure that I saw a speech therapist, though. Only I lied to the therapist about what was causing my anxiety and making me stutter. I said that I was worried about keeping my grades up and getting into a good college."

"I get that. I do." Wade kept her in his arms, warm and tight. "I never told anyone that I was being bullied, either. My stepdad thought I was the one causing trouble, especially after I got suspended. The only good thing for me at that damned school was meeting you."

"And now we're here together." She pressed her ear closer to his chest, to his heart.

He heaved a rugged sigh. "I still have about an hour before I have to leave. I wonder what we should do to kill the time."

"Yes, I wonder." She rolled over, perching herself above him. The sheet that had been draped over her fell away, leaving her completely naked to his view. He was bare, too, and so deliciously handsome.

She lowered her head, eager for a kiss and ready to enjoy the next sinful hour, keeping busy with him.

After Wade was gone, Bailey spent the rest of the morning missing him—and stressing about seeing her mom.

Finally, she got ready to go. Normally, she breezed in late to her mom's, but today she decided to be on time, if not a little early.

She arrived at the French Colonial mansion, a sprawling eighteen-bedroom home that sat on five beautifully manicured acres. There was even a garden maze, a replica of the labyrinth of Versailles. Inside the home, the decor was ridiculously ornate.

As a kid, Bailey had hated living there. To her, it had always felt like a museum to be admired but not touched. She'd gotten past that once by coloring on a Louis XIV–style console table, trying to make the table her own. As punishment, she'd been sent to her room without dessert for a full week, an outright horror, she supposed, for a rebellious six-year-old obsessed with sweets. By the second day, her dad had sneaked cookies to her, and she'd munched them in bed with the covers drawn over her head, feeling wildly triumphant.

Bailey cleared her mind. A new maid, someone she barely knew, answered the door and escorted her to the front parlor to wait for her mom. They always convened in this room. The console table was still there. She smiled to herself. Too bad she didn't have some crayons in her purse, just to give it another go. Her smile quickly fell. Her dad wasn't here to sneak her more cookies, so it wouldn't be the same.

In hindsight, neither of her parents had gotten the parenting thing quite right. Her dad had given her whatever she wanted, and her mom had been too self-absorbed to notice. If it hadn't been for the housekeepers and chefs and maintenance crews who'd taken Bailey under their wing, she wouldn't have learned to become the woman she was today.

While she waited, she sat in a stiff armchair with a gilded frame, fussing to get comfortable. She would never understand her mom's butt-numbing taste in furniture.

A soon as her mother entered the room, Bailey popped up and smoothed her clothes, with an immediate sense of being unkempt.

As usual, Eva Mitchell was the epitome of perfection. She sported a silky blouse paired with slim black slacks from heaven only knew what fashion house. Her tasteful jewelry was rose gold, and her platinum-bleached hair skimmed her shoulders in an elegantly coiffed style. In her heyday, she'd fit the mold of the blonde bombshells who'd come before her, wearing skimpy clothes and pouting at the camera. But now she carried herself like a Beverly Hills socialite.

She still had the figure of a goddess, thanks to her strict eating habits and yoga regimen. She cheated, too, with plastic surgery. Not just on her body, but on her face, as well. She had no intention of looking old, even if time would eventually catch up with her.

"Hello, my darling," Mom said, ever the movie star. "I'm so glad to see you. You look cute. A little flushed, maybe."

Cute? Flushed? Bailey was wearing thrift-store jeans and a classic white T-shirt, with barely any makeup. "I look like I always do."

Mom angled her head. "No. There's something different today."

Maybe it was Wade's effect on her, Bailey thought, and the nonstop sex she'd been having. But she certainly wasn't going to tell her mother that. "I have something important I want to discuss with you. But maybe I should pour us a drink first." The shiny glass bar was just few feet away.

"I'll just have some apple juice," her mother replied.

"I will, too." Bailey decided that alcohol probably wasn't in her best interest, not after the margaritas she'd downed with Wade last night.

She poured two glasses of juice, over ice, and handed one to her mom. Eva was used to having people wait on her. She didn't seem to think twice about it.

They sat across from each other in clock-ticking silence. They'd never had much to say to each other.

Bailey sipped her drink and glanced down at her feet. Along with her jeans and T-shirt, she wore leather sandals. But now she noticed that her toenail polish was chipped. Her mom wouldn't be caught dead without a pristine pedicure.

But Bailey wasn't Eva. They couldn't be more different from each other. She wished, though, that she had inherited just a bit of her mom's striking beauty. Bailey was six inches shorter with a skinny little body and average features. But Wade thought she was beautiful—a fairy, no less—so that was pretty damned cool.

"What's going on?" her mom asked. "What do you want to discuss?"

Bailey anxiously replied, "Remember when I told

you about my Free Your Heart Foundation? Well, it's getting closer to being launched. I was even offered an estate in Pasadena to use for the education center." She went on to explain, finally ending with, "The man who's donating it wants me to host a Hollywood fund-raiser, a fancy ball, so he can meet you. Without your involvement, I won't be able to secure the property."

"Oh my goodness. Really? He's a fan?"

"Apparently so. His name is Gordon Scott, and he's a real estate tycoon. A decent guy, or so I've been told. I haven't met him yet. But he's in his eighties, so he won't run you too ragged on the dance floor."

Her mother laughed. "I'd be honored to meet him and secure the property for you. If you'd like, I can help you host the ball and make it a star-studded event."

"Thank you." She could see how pleased her mom was to be so important in all this. But now came the difficult part. Bailey blew out a breath, struggling to keep her nerves from betraying her. "I need to fill you in on something else, though." She paused, a surge of adrenaline rushing through her. "The bullying I suffered in school was worse than I led you to believe. Mostly, I was harassed for being your daughter. The other kids tormented me because I was short and shy and awkward, and you were sleek and sexy and appearing in men's magazines. The only guys who ever asked me out just wanted to get a hot-and-hungry glimpse of my MILF mom." She winced at the look of horror on her mother's face, but it was too late to backpedal now, so she said, "There was also a half-naked picture of me that was circulated around." She went on to detail the ugly photo Shayla had taken. "My stuttering was the result of the bullying, too. But I hid my anxiety from just about everyone, especially you and Dad."

"I'm so sorry." Her mother heaved a sigh. "I wish we had known. Your daddy would've marched down to that school and made things right."

"He had a lot of other things on his mind then. But I agree, if I'd told him what was going on, it would've helped my situation."

"Well, at least you're telling me now." Mom sipped her apple juice and glanced out the window, staring into space. Was she as disturbed by all of this as she seemed? Or was she just trying to block everything out?

Bailey said, "Just so you know, I'm going to write an essay on the Free Your Heart blog with things that happened to me."

Mom's horrified expression came back. "Do you really think that's necessary? Can't you just say that you were picked on when you were young and leave it at that? I'd rather not have the world know the things that were done to you. Or that they were done, in part, because of me. That just sullies everything even more."

"I suspected that you'd feel that way. At first, I

did, too. But then it struck me that I needed to come clean, not just to you, but publicly, too, for the sake of all the other bullied kids out there going through it as we speak. It's an epidemic, and I want to help put an end to it, however I can."

Her mom covered her face with her hands, lightly, quickly. "People are going to think I was a horrible mother for not knowing what was going on."

"You couldn't have known the whole story, not unless I told you, and it was just too complicated for me back then."

"It's still going to make me look bad."

Seriously? "This isn't about you."

"Oh, I know. But I'm ashamed that you didn't feel comfortable coming to me with your problems. Was I a terrible mother, Bailey? Am I still?"

"Of course not." Bailey had a hand in their fractured relationship, too. "But it's still been tough, trying to connect with you."

"I'm sorry if I didn't support you the way I should have. But with as close as you were to your dad, I always thought that he was enough for you."

"It would be great if you supported me now and stood by me when I write the essay. Maybe you can write one, too, from the parent's perspective, and tell your side of it."

"Yes. I can totally do that. I can explain how, as parents, we're sometimes so busy building our own lives that we don't see what's happening to our children, and they end up suffering because of it. I can encourage parents to look closer at their children and ask questions. And if they suspect that something is wrong, then do something about it."

"That's perfect." So incredibly prefect. Bailey couldn't have asked for a better gift. "As beloved as you are, your voice will reach a lot of people. And with us doing this together, it'll send a message of hope."

"I'm so glad I can help." Mom fanned her face as if she might tear up. "It's just too bad you can't call out your old bullies by name."

"I could. But I'm not going to. I'd rather leave it up to them to come forward, if they have a mind to." Bailey stood and finished her juice. Her legs were actually a little wobbly, but she figured it was from her emotions and the adrenaline leaving her body. "I should go now. I've had a busy weekend."

"Busy how?" Mom stood, as well. "Was there a man involved? Is that why you seem so different?"

"There is someone," Bailey hastily admitted. "But he's just a friend."

"And a bedfellow, I suspect. I'm good at detecting that." Her mother gave her a sly look. "Will I be able to meet him?"

"Eventually. He's helping with the foundation, too. He was my savior in high school. He protected me the best he could."

"Then I want to meet him for sure, and thank him for being kind to my little girl."

Bailey smiled at her mom. She even reached forward for a well-intentioned hug. This was by far the warmest conversation they'd ever had. The calmest, too, without the usual argument between them.

Was this a new day, a new dawn, the future of things to come? If it was, they were off to a wonderful start.

Seven

Bailey was actually enjoying being on a private plane. She was able to relax, so different from when she used to travel with her parents. And there wouldn't be any paparazzi on the ground waiting to pounce.

Wade's pilot was a middle-aged man with salt-and-pepper hair and a classy demeanor. There was no way he was going to gossip about his boss. But Wade claimed that there wasn't much to tell, anyway.

Was that true? Wade didn't talk about himself, at least not in the way Bailey had been doing. He knew practically everything about her family, and she barely knew anything about his. She didn't even know if he was still in touch with his stepfather or if his biological father had ever been part of his life. His mother had passed away prior to him coming to Bev West, but he never really talked about her, either.

She decided that she would ask him more about his family this weekend and see if he had any pictures that he was willing to share. She would love to see what his mom looked like. He'd certainly seen plenty of photos of her mom. Eva was all over the internet. Information about Bailey's dad was available online, too.

Maybe that's what fascinated her about Wade's family. You couldn't just google them to find out who they were. You had to dig deeper, and Bailey loved unearthing people's pasts. To her, it felt like a fascinating form of research. One of her favorite aspects of writing was creating backstories for her characters, and learning about real people helped inspire her work. Too bad that Wade wasn't interested in having his life mapped out in a movie. Writing a screenplay about him would be thrilling. Everything about him enthralled her.

She glanced over at the flight attendant, a blond and bearded twentysomething who'd been seeing to her needs. He was the pilot's son, as it turned out. They worked as a team. He seemed like a classy guy, too. He'd introduced himself as Dax. His father's name was Ken.

As for the jet, it was designed for comfort, with big, cushy seats, a small but elegant dining room and a luxurious bedroom in back. She assumed that

Wade slept there when he was going abroad or taking longer flights.

And what about his former lovers? Had they ever traveled with him? And if so, what were they like? Surely Dax and Ken would know the answers to her questions. But she couldn't bug them about it. Whatever Bailey wanted to know about Wade, she would just have to ask him herself.

Clearing her mind, she sipped her wine and nibbled on the fruit-and-cheese platter Dax had provided.

After he refilled her glass, she got up and headed to the rear of the cabin, where the bedroom was. She'd already been informed that the bed was at her disposal. Of course, it seemed pointless to try to nap, especially since the entire fight was only an hour or so. It took longer than that for her to fall asleep at home. Still, she wanted to get closer to the bed and imagine sharing it with Wade. She'd never had sex on a plane. She wasn't part of the mile-high club.

But what about Wade? Had he done it here before?

She closed the door and sat on the edge of the mattress. If she was braver, she would lie down, lift her dress and touch herself, slipping her hand down her panties. She'd worn a pair of pretty pink boy shorts just for Wade.

Would they mess around as soon she got to his house? Or would it happen later that night?

She glanced around the cream-colored bedroom, drinking her pinot noir and thinking sexy thoughts about her lover. But good girl that she was, she kept her hands out of her panties.

A short time later, she returned to her seat, anxious for the flight to end so she could see Wade. He wasn't picking her up at the airport, though. He'd arranged for a driver.

Trying to keep busy, she opened her e-reader. But her thoughts kept drifting to Wade. She hoped that her compulsion would go away soon. Not too soon. But eventually, she wanted to be able to get through a day without obsessing over him. In some ways, it felt like a loss of her independence, and that scared her more than anything.

That, and falling in love. But she didn't need to worry about love. She wasn't going to lose her heart. But her body? She was already losing that battle.

By the time the plane landed, the ebook she'd been reading was a blur, with a plot she couldn't recite. Her concentration was shot. She just needed to see Wade. For now, nothing else would do.

Dax offered to walk her to the terminal and escort her to the shiny black town car waiting to whisk her away. The driver was female, a curvy brunette, and from the looks she and Dax exchanged, Bailey suspected that they'd spent a night or two together. Dang, how hot was that? Bailey and Wade weren't the only couple having an affair.

The driver introduced herself as Lorna and opened the door for Bailey. She climbed into the back seat and peered out the tinted windows, watching Lorna and Dax give each other one last look before he retreated.

Lorna put Bailey's luggage in the trunk and got behind the wheel. Bailey wished she could ask her about Dax. How long had they known each other? How long had they been sleeping together? Was she obsessed with him? But she couldn't pepper the other woman with questions like that. It would be downright rude. Not to mention presumptuous.

As the car left the curb, Bailey asked, "Are you Wade's regular driver?" At least she could inquire about that.

"Sometimes," Lorna replied. "He has several of us on call." The brunette glanced in the rearview mirror. "Did you have a good flight?"

"Yes, it was nice," she replied, keeping her side of the conversation as proper and polite as Lorna's.

Nonetheless, she still wondered about the affair she assumed Lorna and Dax were having. But she would do well to quit thinking about someone else's sex life, especially since she was engaged in her own wild fling. She squeezed her thighs together, immersed in the anticipation of spending the weekend with Wade.

Bailey silently peered out the window, taking in the scenery. Although she'd been to a few writers' conferences in San Francisco, she didn't know the city all that well.

About forty minutes later, after a bout of heavy traffic, Lorna parked in front of Wade's mansion.

Bailey studied it through the glass. The three-story structure looked like a Victorian castle with its gingerbread details and soft gray trim. An imposing wrought-iron fence surrounded the entire property, but she could still see the courtyard and how lush the grounds were. She also noticed how big his garage was, but Wade had already told her that he had lots of cars. Obviously, he used drivers when he needed them, too.

Lorna sent a text, letting Wade know that she'd arrived. Soon he appeared on the porch, and the front gate creaked open. Still gazing out the window of the car, Bailey watched him.

He looked casual amid the elegance, wearing faded jeans, a simple button-down shirt and leather sneakers. His hair was combed back in its usual style. She was attired in a summer dress and a denim jacket. She'd tried to prepare for the weather—San Francisco wasn't as warm as Los Angeles in the summer. Today the wind was acting up.

He approached the car and opened Bailey's door. She got out and stared straight at him. His lips curved into an appreciative smile, and her heart jumped to her throat.

Lorna exited the car and removed Bailey's luggage. Wade turned and thanked her, letting her know he would take over from there. The driver nodded and disappeared back into her car.

As soon as Lorna was gone, Wade grabbed Bailey

and kissed her, leaving her breathless when it was over. She could do little more than blink.

While she was still recovering, he lifted her suitcase and said, "Come on, I'll show you around."

She nodded and followed him into the courtyard and onto the porch. He closed the gate by remote control with his phone. Was he using a system he'd designed? Most of Wade's success had come from the software he developed and the start-ups he invested in, but Bailey suspected that the work he did with the government was the most fulfilling, especially after his history with the FBI.

They entered his home, and she removed her jacket and hung it on a coatrack in the entryway, where dark woods and stained-glass windows made a powerful statement.

As did the rest of the mansion. The main level featured two turn-of-the-century parlors, a brightly lit living room, a traditional dining room and a sparkling kitchen. A sunny breakfast nook overlooked a brick-and-concrete patio.

The lower level offered a media room, a bonus room and bar, an indoor spa and pool, two changing rooms, and a full bath. The staff's quarters were on the property, too, in an apartment out back, with its own lovely yard.

In the main house, all the bedrooms were upstairs, except for Wade's. His suite dominated the lower level. It also included an adjoining office, a fully equipped gym and a bathroom with his and hers amenities. An etched glass door led to the indoor pool.

"This is incredible," she said. "I love that you have a view of the pool. I've always enjoyed swimming indoors."

"We can swim anytime you want." He placed her luggage near a walk-in closet and turned to look at her. "I'm so glad you're here."

She met his gaze, still reeling a bit from his kiss. "So am I." For now, she wouldn't want to be anywhere else. "I thought about you while I was on the plane."

He moved closer. "Thought about me how?"

She responded in detail, decadent as it was. "At first, I wondered if any of your other lovers have traveled with you, or if you ever slept with them there. Then I imagined having sex with you. I even went into the bedroom and fantasized about touching myself." She released the air in her lungs. "But I didn't do it."

"Then maybe I should do it for you." He backed her against the wall where she stood, his hands traveling down her body.

Bailey closed her eyes, more than willing for him to take control. "I wore pink panties for you."

He nuzzled her cheek, his beard stubble rough against her skin. "What made you think I would like pink?"

She opened her eyes, lost in the beauty of him. "I

don't know. But I wore a pink bra, too, and I hardly ever wear matching lingerie."

He reached under her dress, and when he delved into her panties, she let out a soft moan. He traced her heart-shaped pubis right before he worked his magic, rubbing her where it counted, where it felt so damned good, where she was already getting wet.

He continued his naughty foray, and she lifted the hem of her dress and bunched it around her stomach, giving him better access. At this point, her underwear was halfway down her legs.

He put his fingers deep inside, then brought them up to his mouth. She shivered, watching him.

"I think I better do this the right way." He dropped to his knees, removed her shoes and pulled her panties all the way off.

In her excitement, she tugged her dress over her head, getting rid of it, too. All that was left was her bra. But she left that on. He stood and scooped her up, and she assumed he was going to carry her to his big, opulent bed. But he approached the nearest piece of furniture, a nice little accent table, and placed her on it.

He returned to his knees and positioned himself, encouraging her to lift her legs onto his shoulders. There was no time to be shy. She loved what he was doing and how brazenly he was doing it. She angled her hips and rocked against him.

He pleasured her with masculine fury, with the fever of a man who'd been starving himself just so he could have this moment. Bailey relished the feeling, the heat, the need. She braced her hands against the table, nearly clawing the wood.

Finally, when the intensity became too much to bear, she spiraled into a hot and jerky orgasm.

In the silence that followed, she removed her legs from his shoulders and dangled them over the side of the table, steeped in postclimactic sensations.

He retrieved her panties, stood and handed them to her.

She clutched them between her fingers.

"Just so you know, I do like pink," he said. "Or I like it on you. Thanks for wearing those for me."

Should she thank him for the luscious things he'd just done to her? Somehow, she couldn't quite manage it. She was still a bit dizzy. He helped her off the table, and she tugged the panties into place.

"Another thing," he said. "I have traveled with some of my old lovers, but I've never had sex with any of them on my plane. I've just never been that desperate for anyone." He softly added, "But I'm never going to fly again without thinking about you."

She finally found her voice. "Me, neither. You're probably going to be on my mind whether I'm on the ground or in the air." She pressed her body against his, encouraging him to hold her.

He skimmed a hand down her spine. "I made all sorts of plans for us this weekend."

She gazed up at him. "Besides making me come?"

He toyed with the hooks on her bra. "Yes, besides that. Although I'm not sure how either of us will want to leave the house if you keep tempting me the way you are."

"Then I better get dressed." She couldn't stay in his arms all day, even if she wanted to.

A few hours later, Wade took Bailey out for seafood, and now they strolled along Fisherman's Wharf, surrounded by souvenir shops and food vendors. Tourists flocked to this area, but the locals appreciated it, too. Bailey noticed an eclectic mix of people.

"This is my first time at the wharf," she said. "But it's tough to jam everything into business trips. When I was here with my writers' group, I went to museums and things like that."

"There's a lot to see in this city. But there's a lot to see in most cities. There are still places in LA that I've never been to, and I was born there."

She glanced over at him. "Do you ever miss it?"

He shrugged. "I don't know. Maybe. I definitely liked being in Laurel Canyon with you."

"I liked having you there, too." Hopefully he would come back and stay with her again. She reached for his hand, and they approached the rail that overlooked the water. Sea lions were lounging on a floating dock. "Look at those funny guys."

"Most of them have already migrated south for the summer," he said. "To the Channel Islands to breed. But there's a group that stays behind year-round."

"They're adorable." Just lazing about, napping their time away. "They certainly draw a lot of attention."

"They're known as Sea Lebrities around here."

"Oh, that's cute. Speaking of celebrities, I have some good news to share." News she'd been waiting to tell him. "My conversation with my mother went surprisingly well. She's even going to write an essay, from a parent's perspective, for the Free Your Heart Foundation blog. She's going to help with the Hollywood fund-raiser, too."

"That's great, Bailey. I'm happy for you." His gaze locked onto hers, and he smiled. "That's how it should be."

Although she wanted to ask him about his mother, she refrained. This didn't seem like the appropriate time or place to start a dialogue about his family.

"Have you contacted Gordon yet?" he asked.

"Yes, I did. I emailed him and let him know that I was accepting his offer and that my mom was looking forward to making his acquaintance. I'm going to let him set the date of the fund-raiser, and we'll work to meet his schedule. I think that's only fair since he's donating the property."

"Let me know what he decides, and I'll block out that date on my calendar, too. How's the rest of it going?"

"You mean with the foundation itself? I have lots of volunteers, but I need to hire someone to manage it. I can't do it all myself. But now that things are moving along, I'll be starting the interview process."

"I'm sure you'll find the right person."

"I hope so." She waited a beat before she said, "My mom wants to meet you. I told her you were my savior in high school and that we were hanging out again. She also figured out that we were lovers, so that probably made her even more interested in you. I don't normally bring men home to my family, but you're an old friend, so it's different with you."

"I can meet your mom at the fund-raiser. Or before, if we can swing it."

"I'm just glad that I was honest with her about the bullying. It's a relief that she knows the truth."

He went silent for a second, then asked, "When is she going to write her essay?"

"As soon as I write mine, and I plan on doing that after I get home. It's going to be sort of scary, though, letting the world know what happened to me. But I think it will be freeing, too. That's the reason I named the foundation what I did, so people could free their hearts from whatever pain they endured and reach out to others who've been through it. The name works for anyone who wants to admit that they used to bully someone, too."

"For them to free their hearts?" He blew out a breath. "Not everyone has a heart. Some people are just cruel."

Bailey didn't respond. She was too busy assessing Wade. A faraway look appeared in his eyes, as if he was thinking about someone in particular. But not one of his tormenters from high school. She sensed it was someone altogether different.

He returned his attention to the sea lions, and she wondered if she was reading too much into his expression. Bailey did have a vivid imagination. But she also had an innate ability to read people, and something seemed off.

But again, this wasn't the time to delve into his past. Instead, she went quiet while a breeze brushed past them.

He moved closer to her, and she snuggled deeper into her jacket. He wore a jacket, as well. His was black leather, and it made him look like a bit of a rebel.

They left the sea lions and walked to another pier, stopping to gaze out at the water again. "Is that Alcatraz?"

"Yes, it is."

"Have you ever taken the tour?"

He nodded. "It was surreal, visiting an old federal prison when I'd been in one myself. But weirdly enough, I couldn't seem to resist."

"I don't think I would like it." She thought it looked ominous, even from across the bay. "I'll bet it would be especially gloomy at night."

"I've done both tours, day and night. I even did the behind-the-scenes tour. I took them all, at different times. I'm a glutton for punishment, I guess."

Bailey's mind flew into overdrive. Was the cruel

person he'd been thinking about another inmate? Was his incarceration worse than he'd led her to believe?

"Do you want to get something sweet?" he asked, changing the subject and throwing her off-kilter.

She couldn't think to respond, but thankfully, she didn't have to. He continued with, "It's a little chilly for ice cream, but up ahead is a doughnut shop we can raid."

She forced herself to smile, to act normal. "Sure. That sounds good. My favorite are the glazed. Chocolate frosted are a close second."

"You should get one of each." He softened his voice, almost to a whisper. "Then I can kiss you afterward and taste the glaze and chocolate on your lips."

"You can kiss me whenever you want." She hungered for him as easily as he hungered for her. But that didn't change the fact that her mind was still racing. Or that he was a mystery she'd yet to solve.

Wade made love with Bailey after they returned from the wharf. Then, in the morning, he did it again. He rolled over, got behind her and did wicked things to her hot little body. He couldn't seem to stop himself. He wanted her with a vengeance. Clearly, she wanted him, too. They were in this wild affair together, needing each other in equal measure.

She fell back asleep, and he got up to shower, using the body wash and shampoo she'd made for him. He'd brought them home from her house last week, and every time he lathered with them, he thought of her. Just the scent alone aroused him.

He dried off, got dressed and texted his chef, putting in a breakfast order. For the main entrée, he requested spinach and artichoke omelets, and for the sides, he chose fresh fruit and yogurt parfaits, steel-cut oatmeal and cauliflower hash browns. He figured Bailey would like those combinations. She had the same offbeat appetite as him, sometimes eating healthy and sometimes filling up on junk. Today, he decided, would be a health-conscious day.

By the time the food was delivered, she was awake and wrapped in one of her old-fashioned robes.

They dined by the pool, surrounded by floor-to-ceiling windows and retractable skylights that funneled natural light into the room. Wade thought Bailey looked exceptionally pretty, immersed in the glow, her sleep-tousled hair coiled into a hasty bun. She'd already eaten half of her omelet and was working on the sides.

"This is delicious," she said. "My compliments to the chef. I'm going to have to get the cauliflower recipe from him." She smiled. "Is this breakfast your way of offsetting the doughnuts we had last night?"

"More or less." He smiled, too. "I'll also be taking you out for a nutritious lunch later. I thought we could hang out in Haight-Ashbury and soak up some of that old hippie vibe. There's a lot of vintage stores where you can shop."

"Oh, that's awesome. I wanted to explore that neighborhood when I was here on my own, but I never found the time. My San Francisco trips were always so rushed."

"We'll have all sorts of time today. Also, I was wondering if you'd make more of the body wash and shampoo for me, so I don't run out. You'll probably be able to get the ingredients you need in one of the health stores in the Haight."

"I'd be glad to make you more. But only on one condition. You have to help me wash my hair later."

"Really?" That sounded fascinating, especially with how intrigued he was with the length and volume of her hair. "You've got yourself a deal."

She sipped her orange juice. "Are you driving us to the Haight? And if you are, what car of yours are you taking? You don't have a flower-painted bus, do you?"

"Yes, I'm driving. But I don't have a hippie-mobile." He shrugged, laughed a little. "Maybe I should get one. Then we can ride around like Scooby and the gang."

She broke into a grin. "I loved that cartoon when I was a kid. I actually still like it."

"Me, too. It was my favorite. I loved how they solved all of those silly mysteries."

Bailey turned quiet, and he wondered why her mood had suddenly changed. She seemed distracted. Or reflective or something. She even glanced at her plate without taking another bite.

"What's wrong?" he asked.

"Nothing." She lifted her gaze. "It's just that I was thinking last night when we were at the pier about how you seem like a mystery that I've yet to solve."

He frowned, troubled with the direction she was taking. "There's nothing mysterious about me."

"Are you kidding? You've always been that way, even when we were young. There are so many questions I want to ask you, so much I want to know. But last night, I wondered if your prison experience was worse than you let on and if something bad really did happen to you there."

"Why? Because I took so many tours of Alcatraz?"

"That was definitely part of it. But even before we talked about Alcatraz, you mentioned how cruel people could be, and I got the feeling you were talking about someone specific. But not anyone from our school. It seemed to go beyond that."

"That's not true," he replied, trying to keep himself from panicking. "You're just making stuff up in your head."

"Are you sure? Because if there's something painful that you're hiding, I'll always be here to listen. I know how difficult it is to open up. I just did it with my mom."

"Yeah, but I'm not hiding anything." Except for his whole damned existence, he thought. But he wasn't going to start blabbing about his mother's heartbreak or his father's crimes. Bailey didn't need to know about the shame or the pain or the contamination he'd been trying to wash from his veins.

"I'm sorry. I didn't mean to upset you." She reached for her napkin. "You just confuse me sometimes."

"It's okay." He scooted his chair closer to the table and gazed across the pool. "Don't worry about it." From now on, he was going to have to be extra careful around her. Less transparent and more guarded. Or should he appear less guarded and more transparent, showing her a more relaxed side of himself? He had no idea how to behave to get her off his trail. But he did know how to lie and tell half-truths, and that was what he would continue to do. Because nothing was more important to Wade than protecting his secrets.

Eight

Bailey returned from the Haight with wonderful vintage finds, but her favorite items had come from Wade. He'd purchased a collection of antique hair ornaments for her. Some were simple and others were ornate, with crystals and pearls and colored rhinestones.

After they got settled back into his room and she put everything away, he asked, "When am I going to get to wash your hair?"

"We can do it now if you want." She had a special plan, and it involved more than him just shampooing her hair. "You'll have to get in the shower with me. It's too hard to wash it in the sink or the tub. Unless it's a salon-style sink, and you don't have one of those."

"No, I can't say that I do. But I'm totally onboard with a shower. What shampoo should we use?"

"I brought a bottle that I made for myself. It's lavender and mint." She still had to make more of the one she'd given him, but she could do that later.

"Sounds good." He smiled easily at her.

But was he as relaxed as he seemed? Even after the conversation they'd had earlier, he still puzzled her. He'd insisted that he wasn't hiding anything, yet she wasn't sure if she believed him. His smile seemed like a mask.

Then again, maybe she was being overly dramatic, looking for a trauma that didn't exist. Nonetheless, she still intended to inquire about his family. Just a few questions to satisfy her curiosity and hopefully make him less of a mystery.

Only for now, there was the business of her hair. She removed her shampoo and conditioner from her toiletry case.

They entered his bathroom, and he flipped a switch. Several lights came on, including a black-and-silver chandelier that created an elegant effect.

The shower was equipped with multiple jets, positioned in every direction. They removed their clothes and walked into the marble enclosure. He closed the door and activated the jets, getting both of them wet. She turned around so he could soak her hair with a handheld sprayer, which he did, quite efficiently.

He squeezed a large dollop of shampoo onto his hands and massaged her scalp, treating her with care.

He was good at this. But he was good at everything that involved touching her. He took his time, doing it right.

The scents of lavender and mint swirled through the steam-filled air, intensifying the intimacy while he lathered every long, thick strand of her hair.

She helped him rinse out the shampoo and apply the conditioner. A few minutes later, after the task was complete, she shut off the jets and shifted to face him.

They kissed, soft and slow, and he rubbed his body against hers. He was already half-hard, but that was only the beginning. Bailey ended the kiss and dropped to her knees.

She licked a bead of water that had collected in his navel, and his stomach muscles jumped, his abs tensing and releasing.

"What are you doing?" he asked in a sandpapery voice.

"What you've been doing to me." Was his heart pounding harder? Hers definitely was. She felt it thumping in her chest.

"There's no rule that says you have to—"

"I know, but this was my plan all along."

He ran his thumb across her lips, back and forth, as if he was imagining what came next. "Tricky girl."

She could tell that he was anxious for her to begin, but she teased him, letting the anticipation build. She even turned the shower back on, choosing one lone jet that sprayed his backside. He pitched forward, his erection getting bigger and straining toward her. She leaned closer, and he tangled his hands through her waterlogged hair.

Feeling strong and seductive, she waited another minute, ticking off the seconds in her mind. She loved being on her knees for him.

Finally, she stroked him with her hands and her mouth, making him fully aroused. She controlled the motion, but he participated, too, heightening the rhythm. She glanced up to see if he was watching. He was, ever so intently.

She took him deeper, giving him as much pleasure as possible. He made rugged sounds of excitement. She reached around to grab his ass, marveling at how taut it was. His body mesmerized her. His height. His sinewy muscles.

She glanced up at him again, and they stared at each other.

She could feel the pressure building. He was trying to hold on, to not come so quickly. But she didn't slow the pace. Instead, she increased it, wanting to drive him to the brink of erotic destruction the way he so often did to her.

He fisted handfuls of her hair, tugging on them like reins. She kept bobbing her head, up and down, prompting his climax.

His breath rushed out, and his body jerked, his pelvis thrusting to meet her manipulations.

He didn't spill into her mouth. Somehow, he managed to break free and splash her breasts. Bailey closed her eyes, almost as if she was coming, too.

Sticky with his warmth, she got up off her knees and turned on the rest of the shower jets. As she washed off, he pulled her into his arms and kissed her hard and fast, letting her know just how much he appreciated her effort to please him.

On Sunday afternoon, Wade took Bailey back to the waterfront, only this time they explored the sea life at the Aquarium of the Bay. After that, they rode the carousel at the pier as an homage to the merry-go-round they'd ridden together at their class reunion.

In the evening, they went to Chinatown to eat and shop, and she came back with all sorts of goodies, including an antique teakettle to add to her collection at home. Wade had never known anyone who collected so many different things.

"I'm having a wonderful time," she said as she placed her wares on the bed. "Good thing I took your private jet or I would've had to buy an extra suitcase for all the stuff I got."

He nodded. She was going home tomorrow morning, and he would miss the hell out of her when she was gone. "What should we do now? Listen to music, stream a movie, go for a swim?"

"Let's swim." She quit fussing with her purchases. "I haven't been in your pool yet, and it's one of my favorite things about your house." She sat on the edge of the bed. "Plus, I brought this great little retro bathing suit with me."

He was going to suggest that they swim naked, but if she wanted to show off her swimsuit, then he would wear his, too.

They changed in front of each other, and he smiled when he got a gander at her suit, a modest two-piece with a ruffly top and high-waisted bottoms. She looked adorable.

"Check this out." She produced a multicolored swim cap adorned with faux flowers. She plunked it on her head to model it.

He smiled again. She was definitely one of a kind. "That's quite a novelty. But is all of your hair going to fit under that thing?" For now, her braid hung out the back.

"It'll fit. Besides, it'll keep my hair from getting wet. It just takes so long to dry. You know, you helped me dry it yesterday after our shower."

Yeah, he had. And she was right, it took forever. But that wasn't the part of their shower experience that stuck out in his mind.

They entered the pool area. The windows and skylights were open, but it was night, so darkness formed the backdrop. Inside the room, LED lights created a colorful glow.

Bailey tucked her braid under the cap, and when she dived into the water, he watched her. She swam as well as any of the marine life they'd seen at the aquarium.

After a few minutes of admiring her backstroke, he dived in after her, and they played like a couple of friendly fish, swimming in and around each other. They came up for air and kissed a few times.

A short while later, they dried off, and he fixed drinks at the poolside bar. They sat in lounge chairs and sipped chocolate martinis, getting their sweet tooths on.

"This is yummy," she said, toasting him with it.

"Glad you like it." He studied her, all wrapped up in her towel. Her braid was free. She'd ditched the kitschy swim cap. "Chef left some snacks for us in the fridge if we get hungry later."

"I'm good for now. I'm still full from dinner."

"Me, too." But he wanted to be sure that she was well-fed on this trip and that he was a proper host.

They both were silent for a while, just sipping their drinks. Then she said, "I hope you don't mind if I ask you something."

He didn't know if he was going to mind, not until she elaborated. But he suspected that it was going to be of a personal nature, and he never liked that. "What do you want to know?"

"Do you have any old pictures that I can see? I've been wondering what your mom looked like."

Damn. There she went, delving into what she obviously thought was part of his mystery. Only now it involved his family. The true nature of his pain.

He replied, "I don't have any pictures handy. Everything from my youth is in storage." He just couldn't bear to keep that stuff around. "I resemble her a bit. Or my eyes do, anyway." Other than that, he favored the prick who'd fathered him.

"What sort of work did she do?"

"She was a hairdresser when I was little. She wanted to open her own salon, but it never happened." Wade's dad had stolen the money she was supposed to use for her business. He taken every last dime of an inheritance that she'd received from her deceased parents. "She quit doing hair when I got older and managed a beauty supply shop."

"Oh, wow. I never would've guessed that your mom worked in that industry. But it makes sense, as fascinated with hair as you are."

"I'm only fascinated with yours." He didn't usually chase women around for their long, luscious locks.

"Well, it still seems to make some sort of sense to me. And I'm so sorry that you lost your mom. I remember you saying in high school that she passed away not long before we'd met."

"It was tough. She had a kidney infection that caused sepsis. She didn't get treated early enough for the infection, the way she should've. Sometimes she got depressed and didn't look after herself. She had a fragile nature." He could hardly believe that he was saying these things out loud, telling Bailey about his mother in a way that made him vulnerable, too. "I grieved something awful when she was gone. So did Carl."

"Carl? Is that your stepfather?"

"Yeah. He's gone, too. He died when I was in prison."

"Oh my goodness. And here I've been wondering if you've remained in touch with him or if he still lived in LA. I assumed he was still around."

"He had cancer, but I didn't know about it until after he was gone." Once again, Wade realized he was putting himself in a vulnerable position by admitting all this. But if he didn't satisfy Bailey's interest in his family, she would probably keep questioning him. He figured it was better to give her some of the story, difficult as it was. "Carl and I were never really close, but I think he did his best to parent me. This is awful, but I ignored his letters before he died. I wouldn't let him visit me, either."

She gave him a concerned expression. "Why not?"

"I was still mad over some of our old arguments. But then I never got the chance to make things right. If I'd been aware of his illness, I would have seen him, for sure. I have no idea why he kept his diagnosis from me. But I do know that he was kind and patient with my mother. They were friends before they got married, and he understood her a lot better than I did." Because Carl had known the truth all along about Wade's dad. "Anyway, that's pretty much it. My family in a nutshell."

She set her drink aside. "What about your biological father? Where does he fit into the equation?"

Wade collected his thoughts. He'd already said

more than he'd expected to say, and by no means was he going to open up about the bastard who'd spawned him. But if he shut down completely, would Bailey get suspicious? Damn, but he hated being in this position, picking and choosing what tidbits were safe to reveal.

"I have no idea who my dad is," he said, starting with what used to be the truth. "All my mom ever said about him was that he was gone, and that he never knew I existed. I assumed she meant that he was dead, but I never asked. I could tell that she didn't want to talk about him."

Bailey cocked her head. "She never told you his name?"

"No." He'd learned it later on from Carl. And by now, he knew his old man's inmate ID number, too. He'd memorized the damned thing, just as he'd memorized the one that used to belong to him. But at least they hadn't been incarcerated in the same institution. Wade had been sent to what was sometimes referred to as a federal prison camp, with fewer guards and more freedom, whereas his dad was being housed in a medium-security facility with fewer privileges and cage-style rooms.

Bailey frowned a little. Were the wheels in her head turning? Was she going to keep pressing the issue?

Sure enough, she was.

"Are you curious about him?" she asked.

He hastily replied, "I was when I was young. But now that I'm older, it doesn't matter."

"I wonder if he was a one-night stand, and that's why your mom described him as being gone and why he never knew about you. If they had a relationship and he died, I think she would've told you more about him. Unless it was really tragic, and she couldn't bear it."

Wade downed the rest of his frilly martini, wishing that he'd mixed something stronger. "You don't need to go into writer mode about this. What's done is done. My mom is gone, and so is the guy who impregnated her."

"I'm sorry. I wasn't trying to be insensitive. I appreciate you telling me about your mom." Bailey left her lounger and scooted next to him on his. "I think she would have been proud of the man you've become."

"She would be happy about my success." But he suspected that she would be devastated by how much he hated his dad. According to Carl, his mom had never stopped loving his dad and had always hoped that he would redeem himself someday.

Bailey put her hand against his jaw. "I wish I could've known her."

"She would've liked you." He didn't want to keep talking about this. He needed a reprieve, but he needed Bailey, too. He leaned toward her. "Can we forget this now?"

"Forget it how?"

In every way he could, he thought. "I just want to go to bed. With you. Right now."

She didn't respond. Instead, she kissed him, making him want her even more. So much so, he stood and scooped her into his arms, carrying her straight to his room.

He set her on her feet, and they peeled off their swimsuits, leaving them on the floor. He caressed her, filling his hands with her flesh, her gentle curves, her pointy pink nipples. He sought her mouth for another kiss, and they sank onto the bed, practically melding into each other.

Could his heart race any faster? Could his body ache any more than it already was? She rubbed him where it hurt, and he got big and hard, so damned eager for her. A knot of anticipation burned in his blood, spreading like wildfire.

With an aroused shiver, she opened her thighs and invited him inside. He took her quickly, thrusting long and deep. She dug her nails into his shoulders, and his blood burned even hotter. The dance of lovers. The mindless euphoria. She smelled like perfume and pool water, and he was drowning in it.

He stayed on top, where he could control the pressure, the rhythm, the speed. But once would never be enough. He was going to make them both come, then do it again. As many times as it took to satisfy the craving—if it could be satisfied at all.

Bailey awakened early, and since Wade was still asleep, she got up and went into the bathroom to mix the shampoo and body wash she'd promised to make. She'd gotten sidetracked last night by all the sex. Hot, wild, breathtaking sex.

She wished that she didn't have to go home today. All she wanted was more and more of Wade. But she had to return to her regularly scheduled life, at least until the next time she saw him. She was glad that he'd opened up to her about his family. Slowly but surely, she was chipping away at the mystery that was Wade. Or she hoped that she was. He still seemed lost. But what did she expect? He'd survived a lot of pain.

"Bailey?" His voice came out of nowhere, giving her a start. She glanced at the mirror and saw him standing behind her, with his hair falling forward and his boxers slung low on his hips. She was in her underwear, too.

"Hi," she said. She'd left the bathroom door open. As big as his suite was, she hadn't stopped to think that her task would've disturbed him. "I didn't mean to wake you. I forgot to make this yesterday."

"It's okay." He frowned at his own reflection. "It was weird waking up and not having you there. But I guess I'll have to get used to that once you're gone."

She would have to get used to it, too, even if all she wanted was to be near him. "I still need to pack, too."

"I'm sorry that I can't drive you to the airport. I have a business meeting, and I'd never make it back in time."

"It's okay. Lorna can take me. Or whoever my

driver will be today." She met his gaze in the mirror. "Why didn't you pick me up when I arrived? Why did you send a driver then?"

He pushed his hair away from his forehead. "I had some work I was wrapping up that day, too."

She met his gaze in the mirror. "I think Lorna and Dax are having an affair."

"Really?" He sounded surprised. "What makes you think that?"

"It was the way they looked at each other. It's a lot like how we look each other."

"Then maybe they are. But I try not to get involved in my employees' personal lives." He moved forward, pressing the front of his body to the back of hers. "I have enough madness of my own."

"Likewise." He drove her beautifully mad, too. He slipped his arms around her waist, and she glanced at his wrist. "Maybe I should get a tattoo like yours. Well, not exactly like yours, but something that defines me."

He smiled. "You can have my name inked on your butt."

She laughed. "Yes, because no one ever regrets putting their lover's name on their body."

"Maybe I should write it on you with a permanent marker."

"It wouldn't be permanent on my skin. It would wash off eventually."

"Let's do it and see how long it lasts." He nipped

at her earlobe. "But not on your butt. You won't be able to see it there."

"Then where?" Intrigued by his game, she was willing to let him write it wherever he wanted it to go.

"Let me get the marker first, then I'll decide."

He left the room, and she remained by the bathroom mirror, eager for his return.

He came back with a fine-point marker. She turned around to face him, and they stared longingly at each other. Would she ever get enough of him? Would the madness ever end?

"Let's just keep it simple." He took her arm and printed "Wade" on her wrist, in the same exact spot where his tattoo was on him. "Now we're the same."

Except that his design was computer code, and hers was name of the man she was sleeping with. "Maybe you should add a flower or something to it."

"How about this?" He drew a black heart, filling it in, making it stand out.

She nearly swooned like a schoolgirl. But she wasn't worried that the heart was a prelude to love. She knew it represented passion. The heat that never seemed to fail them.

In the next desperate minute, she kissed him. He dropped the marker, and it rolled onto the floor. She almost wished the tattoo was real. But for now, she would take whatever passion she could get, for however long it lasted.

Nine

Over the next three weeks, the fund-raiser efforts flew into high gear. First up, Bailey hired a whiz kid to manage the foundation, a brand-new college graduate who was turning into a godsend. But her mom proved invaluable, too. They'd both written and published their essays, which marked the official launch of the Free Your Heart cause. Mom's essay went viral, hitting the celebrity news outlets, drawing all sorts of attention to the foundation.

Bailey had even received a private email from Shayla Lewis this afternoon. Yep, her old high school bully. Shayla wanted to meet for coffee tomorrow. She hadn't given a reason, but Bailey hoped that it involved an apology.

Either way, Bailey had already texted Wade about it. Due to work conflicts, they hadn't seen each other since her San Francisco trip. He would be visiting this weekend, though, and she couldn't be happier.

But for now, she was at her mom's mansion. They shared a blue velvet settee, paging through a book about historical fashions. Mom had come up with a Victorian theme for the ball and insisted on having their gowns made. They were using the book's etchings from the 1830s through the 1890s for reference.

"I don't see why I can't rent a costume," Bailey said. "Or get something ready-made." She'd seen lots of retailers on the internet that sold Victorian-style gowns.

"You should wear something original, not something anyone else can rent or buy. This is your coming-out party, darling. Your first Free Your Heart fund-raiser." Mom pointed to a drawing of a taffeta gown with a dramatic bustle. "You'd look gorgeous in something like this."

Gorgeous? Her mom had never used that word to describe her before. It made her feel all warm and fuzzy inside. But more importantly, they were spending quality time together. "That is quite a dress." Big and poufy with yards of lace. "But I think it might overwhelm me. I prefer slimmer silhouettes." She gestured to a picture of a dress with a softer bodice and narrower skirt. "Maybe something along these lines?"

"Here's a thought. Why don't we shop for an authentic Victorian gown for you, with the silhouette you prefer? You already wear a lot of vintage things, so why not go for the real deal for the fund-raiser? I can have my stylist hunt up some dresses for you to try. I'm sure she has lots of resources for antique clothes."

"That would be wonderful." Bailey loved the idea of donning an old gown. "But even if she finds one that suits me, it'll probably need to be altered to fit."

"Don't worry about the details. I'll take care of everything. I want my baby girl to be the belle of the ball." Mom closed the book and placed it on a marble table next to the settee. "Why don't I recall helping you choose your prom dress?"

"Because I didn't go to prom."

"You didn't? Mercy." Mom pursed her shiny red lips. "Why didn't I know that?"

"You were out of town on a magazine shoot at the time, traveling to different locations. And by the time you got back, your mind was still somewhere else."

"On my career, as usual. I'm so sorry I wasn't there when you needed me."

"You're here now." And that meant everything to Bailey. "Besides, I wouldn't have attended my prom even if you'd been available to help me choose a dress. It's water under the bridge."

"No, it's not. Things like that matter." Mom shifted in her seat. "It's too bad you and Wade didn't date in high school. He should've been your prom date."

"He'll be escorting me to the fund-raiser. I can't

believe it's only a month away. My head is already spinning."

"Mine, too. But it's been so much fun for me. So, when I am going to get to meet Wade? I was hoping to have already met him by now."

Bailey smiled. "He's coming to see me this weekend. I'll be sure to introduce you then."

"You glow when you talk about him. You absolutely shine." Mom leaned a little closer. "I think you're falling in love."

Oh my God. Bailey shook her head. She'd already discounted that possibility, numerous times. "That's nonsense. We're just friends."

"He's the most important lover you've ever had."

"Yes, but sex isn't love." She clutched her stomach. She was getting butterflies, but that didn't mean anything. She always got fluttery over Wade, and she was excited about seeing him this weekend. "I'm not the type, and neither is he."

"Well, you're certainly behaving like a woman in love, and I'm a bit of an expert in that regard. I might be oblivious to other things, but love isn't one of them."

"You're wrong." And Bailey wasn't going to be persuaded otherwise. Her mom used to ignore her, and now she was conjuring up things that weren't there. "I know my own mind."

"But do you know your own heart?"

"Of course I do." At this point, Bailey wanted to get up and walk out, storming off the way she normally did when they disagreed. But she kept her cool. They were just starting to build a rapport, and the last thing they needed was to fight.

Thankfully, her mom changed the subject, taking the pressure off. But Bailey still had those danged butterflies. And why wouldn't she? In spite of the unnerving love talk, she was still eager to see Wade.

The following day, Bailey sat outdoors with Shayla, sipping gourmet coffee beneath an umbrella-shaded table at a sidewalk café. Shayla had chosen the upscale location. She looked right at home in the elite Hollywood setting, with her poised posture and monochromatic outfit. But was it all just a facade?

Bailey was beginning to wonder why the other woman had arranged this meeting. So far, she hadn't said anything of substance.

Then, finally, it happened. Shayla frowned at the lipstick mark on her cup and said, "I read the essay you wrote."

Bailey merely nodded. "And what did you think of it?"

The brunette glanced up. "It made me nervous. I kept expecting to see my name in it."

"I had no intention of doing that."

Shayla leaned forward in her chair. "Why not?"

"Because I didn't write it to call you out. I did it for my own healing and to help anyone else who's being bullied."

"I'm still worried that someone from Bev West

will come forward and say that it was me. And if that happens, my reputation will be damaged and my business could suffer. We're living in a cancel culture now, and I can't afford to lose my livelihood over this."

Bailey raised her eyebrows. "You invited me to coffee because you're worried about yourself? I was hoping for an apology."

"I do want to apologize. But I don't really know how." Shayla cut into the carrot-quinoa muffin she had yet to eat. "Should I write one of those essays, too? Should I come forward before someone mentions my name?"

She still sounded as if she was more concerned about herself than she was about being sorry. "Are you comfortable about sharing your story? Because once you do, there's no taking it back."

"I know, but I'm already in too deep to walk away. My husband didn't know that I humiliated people when I was young. He was shocked when I told him that the mean girl in your essay was me." She picked at the muffin. "He remembers seeing you and Wade at the reunion. But he didn't know there was bad blood between us. He didn't hear what you and Wade were saying to me. But honestly? The only reason I confided in him was because I thought it would be worse if he found out on his own. Your foundation is getting a lot of buzz, and I've been sitting on pins and needles ever since."

"My mom is the reason our essays got so much

attention. Everything she does causes a stir. But I understand about how tough it was for you to come clean to your husband. I had to do the same thing with my mom."

"I could tell by what she wrote that you're just getting to know each other on a deeper level. I really am sorry that I made high school so awful for you. I'm sorry that I was such a bitch at the reunion, too. You and Wade just seemed so powerful, and I didn't know how to react."

"We were trying to seem that way. We needed to feel strong. He's become a close friend, a lot closer than we were in high school. But we were really troubled back then."

"I'm grateful that I have my husband. Kirk is a wonderful man. We're actually trying to start a family. And now I keep thinking how horrible it would be if someone bullied our child. If he or she went to school every day, hating life. No one has a right to do that to another person."

By now, Bailey believed that Shayla was being sincere. She still might be worried about her reputation, but she also seemed genuinely concerned about a child she hadn't even conceived yet. "If you want to write an essay for the foundation, I'd be more than glad to publish it. I appreciate your apology, and I accept it."

"Thank you." Shayla looked relieved. "Will you say that publicly, too?"

"Yes. I'll stand by your apology. I wouldn't have

created the Free Your Heart Foundation if I didn't want people to free their hearts."

"It's going to be scary putting myself out there. But at least I can take responsibility for my actions, instead of agonizing about them coming back to haunt me." Shayla paused. "I still need to make a donation to your foundation. But I'll do that soon. I heard about the Victorian ball you're hosting. Everyone in town is talking about it."

Was she hoping for a personal invite? Bailey couldn't quite tell. But just in case, she made the offer. "If you and Kirk would like to attend the ball, you're welcome to join us and make your donation that way."

"Thank you. I love a good party. But maybe I better wait to see if my essay is well received. Otherwise, people might trash me at the ball."

"No one is going to bully you at an antibullying event. If anything, they're going to admire you for having the courage to be part of the healing."

"Thank you." The brunette blew out a big windy sigh. "Kirk is going to be happy when I tell him how this meeting went. I'm fortunate to have someone who loves me the way he does. Sometimes I wonder what I did to deserve him."

Bailey didn't want to think about love. Or talk about it. Or imagine how glorious it was supposed to be. Wade would be arriving in two days, and the only thing that mattered was being hot and sexy friends.

Or so she hoped.

* * *

On Saturday afternoon, the sexy-friend thing took a weird turn. Or at least for Bailey. She and Wade were at her mom's mansion, and every so often Mom would shoot her an inquisitive look, making Bailey feel as if she was under a microscope.

Was her mother judging her, searching for what she thought were signs of love? And what about Wade? Could he sense how uncomfortable Bailey was? Or was his mind elsewhere? Mom was chatting about the fund-raiser.

The three of them were gathered for lunch in the rose garden, dining on pan-seared cod and lemon risotto. Bailey glanced at the maze out in the distance. When she was younger, she used to weave in and out of the hedges, pretending that the maze was her own private sanctuary. Later, her brother and Margot had gotten married there, putting a completely different spin on it.

Mom said to Wade, "My stylist is hunting for an antique dress for Bailey to wear to the fund-raiser, scouring the globe for just the right one. What are you planning to wear?"

"I don't know," he responded. "I haven't really thought about it. What types of suits did men wear to formal occasions in the Victorian era?"

"I have a book I can lend you. But I believe that tuxedos with tailcoats were proper attire. Black was the most common color, but the dandy types sometimes wore blue waistcoats. Fancy buttons could be incorporated, as well. A derby hat was optional." Mom dabbed her mouth with a cloth napkin, sitting tall and straight, like the lady of the manor that she was. "For authenticity, you should probably have your outfit custom made."

He replied, "I'll talk to my tailor about it. But I'm not the dandy type, so I'll stick with black. I'd like to see the book you have, though."

"Wonderful. I'll give it to you before you and Bailey go home. Or to her home, as it were. It's so nice that you were able to visit her this weekend, and that you and I had the chance to meet."

Jeez, Bailey thought. Mom was laying it on thick. But sooner or later this lunch would end and Bailey would have Wade all to herself. Still, she was glad that Wade and her mom were getting along. She just wished that Mom hadn't planted that love seed. A seed that wasn't going to grow, she reminded herself. She wasn't falling in love, and it was foolish to keep stressing over it.

As the conversation progressed, Bailey focused on her food. But the lady of the manor kept slanting her sideways glances. Now she was starting to miss the days when her mom used to ignore her. What was that old cautionary saying? *Be careful what you wish for, lest it come true.*

Bailey sighed in relief when dessert was served. She dipped into the watermelon granita. Mostly it was just a slushy in a fancy bowl with a spoon. But it hit the spot, keeping her occupied while the meal wound down.

After lunch, Mom suggested that Bailey and Wade go for a walk in the maze, as if she was some sort of matchmaker and was trying to give them time alone. Nonetheless, Bailey jumped at the chance. She needed to get away.

"This is amazing," Wade said as they strolled in and out of the hedges. "I've never seen anything like it."

Bailey explained, "It's a replica of the labyrinth at Versailles during Louis XIV's reign. Another king had it removed later, replacing it with an English-style garden, but the original design had these same features. The fountains and sculptures represent the fables of Aesop, and the plaques next to them are quatrains written by a seventeenth-century poet."

"Well, it's certainly an interesting concept."

"Louis XIV didn't come up with it on his own. Charles Perrault suggested the Aesop's fables angle. Those fables have been around since ancient Greece."

"And who was Charles Perrault, exactly?"

"He was a French author who published fairy tales that were derived from folktales. He basically laid the foundation for the fairy-tale genre, readapting *Sleeping Beauty* and things like that." She glanced around, taking it all in. "My mom had this labyrinth built to complement the architecture of the house. But it was my hideaway when I was a kid. I loved coming here."

"I can see why. It would be easy to get purposely lost in here." He stopped walking, standing between two sixteen-foot hedges, with a rocaille-decorated fountain up ahead. "Was something going on earlier between you and your mom? You were really quiet over lunch."

Should she tell him what was wrong? The accusation her mother had made? Or would that send the rest of the weekend into a tailspin? Regardless of his reaction, she decided to be honest. She couldn't pretend that nothing was amiss.

"My mom is driving me nuts," she said. "I thought things were improving, but now she's becoming one of those helicopter parents, watching everything I do and meddling in my business."

"That's probably just her way of trying to make up for the past."

"Yes, but she's going overboard. She even thinks that I'm falling in love with you." Before his face blanched, she quickly added, "I told her that you and I are just friends. But she won't listen."

"Damn." He dragged a hand through his hair. A few beats later, he shakily asked, "So, there's absolutely no validity to it? I mean, you don't, you're not…"

"No. Of course not." Bailey refused to feel that way, even if her heart was skipping way too many beats. "You're the most amazing friend and lover I've ever had, but that's not the same as falling in love. I was there when Margot first fell in love with my brother, and it was chaos. That's not what's happening to me." Bailey had moments of weakness, but overall, she still had her wits about her. "I'm stronger than that. But I can't deny that I think about you all the time. In and out of bed."

"I think about you, too. So damned much. I've never had a lover like you before, either." He hesitated. "But you didn't have to tell me what your mom said."

"I know. But I don't want to keep secrets from you." She looked into the vastness of his eyes. "If I lied and said I was fine, instead of admitting that my mom was bugging me about love, it would keep weighing on me, and you'd keep wondering if there was something wrong."

He jammed his hands into his front pockets. "Love scares me. It always has."

"I know. Me, too. But there's no reason for either of us to worry. It's not going to happen to us. We don't have to talk about it anymore, either. We can just move on and forget about it." This conversation was making both of them far too nervous.

He agreed to let it go, and they resumed walking through the maze, trapped within their own anxious minds, where love wasn't supposed to exist.

Ten

Wade shifted on the sofa in Bailey's living room. He was supposed to be searching for something for them to watch, but he couldn't concentrate. He just stared at the channel grids on the TV. Bailey was taking a bath and would join him soon. After the day they'd had, she'd wanted to relax. He did, too. But he wasn't doing a very good job of it. He couldn't get their conversation from earlier off his mind.

Was there a chance that Bailey was falling in love with him? Or that he was having deeper feelings for her? He didn't know squat about love, other than the pain his mom had suffered from it. Either way, he was glad that Bailey didn't want to keep talking about it. He couldn't handle the thought of falling in love. Or of having her falling for him. He wanted to keep things simple.

He almost laughed to himself. There was nothing simple about the fear of love. But what was the point in worrying about it? They were both determined not to let it happen, and that gave him the relief he needed for now. Still, should he own up to his secrets and tell her about his dad? Should he admit how dirty it made him feel or how confused he was that his mom had never stopped loving the con man who'd ripped her off?

He glanced at the television screen, then switched to the streaming channel that offered the old newsmagazine show that featured his dad's victims. He could suggest that he and Bailey watch it tonight. Then, if he felt ready afterward, he could tell her the truth.

He blew out a breath, hoping and praying that he could pull this off. He'd spent so many years protecting his secret, he didn't know how to be honest. But at least he could try.

Anxious to get the damned streaming show going, he waited for her to come into the living room.

She finally appeared, dressed in a T-shirt and drawstring shorts, her hair plaited into a side-swept braid. She smelled sweet and fresh, like flowers and honey. Was it a new body wash she'd made? He liked the aroma. It made him want to strip her bare. But this wasn't the time for sex.

"Did you find something for us to watch?" she asked.

"Sort of. I'm not in the mood for a movie, so I was thinking we could watch a mystery-news show. I found a bunch of them." He zeroed in on his dad's episode. "This one is called *Romeo Ron*, and the synopsis says it's about a group of women who were ripped off by the same guy. But then a mysterious stranger came along and reimbursed the money he'd stolen from them."

"Ooh. That sounds interesting. I'll make some popcorn." She headed for the kitchen.

Wade remained on the sofa, feeling much too jittery. His dad had used aliases, but his real name was Ronald Deacon Jones, hence the "Romeo Ron" title.

A few minutes later, Bailey returned with a big bowl of buttered popcorn and two cans of lemon-flavored water. She set the popcorn on the coffee table and handed him a water.

He thanked her and flipped open the can, eager to take a swig. Anything to calm his nerves. Bailey sat next to him, and he started the show.

According to the program, Wade's dad had refused to be interviewed. But they flashed his picture and gave a bit of background information on him. Bailey commented on how handsome he was. For a second, Wade wondered if she might notice a family resemblance. But even with as much as he favored his father, he wasn't the spitting image of him.

As the story continued, Bailey remarked on how

bad she felt for the women, trusting someone who'd betrayed them. Yeah, Wade felt that way, too. He still ached for his mom, and no one even knew about her link to Ron. No one except for Carl, and he was gone now, too. Wade was the only secret keeper left.

He frowned at the TV. The women in the program were extremely grateful for the benefactor who'd reimbursed what had been stolen from them. But they were stumped by who this anonymous person was and why he or she had taken an interest in Ron's victims.

The episode concluded with how careful the benefactor was to protect his or her identity, using untraceable sources.

Bailey heaved a big sigh. "That was fascinating. It really makes you wonder about the benefactor. Do you think it's someone who found this case randomly? Or do you think there's a deeper connection?"

All Wade had to do was admit that it was him. Just say it. Tell her that Ron was his father. But he clammed up, the words dying in his throat. The fear of opening up was too strong. He wasn't ready to claim those bloodlines. He wasn't ready for anything, apparently. Not love. Not honesty. Not even a true friendship with Bailey. It made him feel awful about himself, but he just couldn't do it.

He lied, as always. "I have no idea how the benefactor got involved, but that was the point of the show, I guess." He swigged the rest of his water, wishing his heart would quit pounding. "It could be anyone."

"Someone who has money. That was a lot of cash to turn over to those ladies. Did you notice how all of the women seemed sort of alike? Not the way they looked, but their mannerisms? Romeo Ron had a type."

Wade's stomach twisted. "Yeah, the type who fell for his charms."

"His background is sad, though. Losing his parents at a young age and then being raised by a controlling uncle."

"That's no excuse for what he turned out to be." Wade refused to feel empathy for his dad.

Bailey gazed at the half-eaten popcorn. "I wonder if he knows who the benefactor is. Or if he's at least thankful that someone helped his victims."

"I doubt he knows who it is." There was no damned way that Ron could know. "As for him being thankful, he's apparently never spoken one way or another about it." To Wade, that was an indication that his dad didn't care. But Wade hadn't reimbursed the money to appeal to his father. He'd done it for the victims, giving them a chance to resume their lives.

Not that his mom had resumed hers. She'd still been in love with his dad when she'd married Carl, and poor Carl had accepted the fact that she would never love him in the way she'd loved the con man who'd fathered her child. Love didn't make sense to Wade, and he doubted that it ever would.

* * *

Later that night, Wade reached for Bailey, and she climbed onto his lap. With her braid falling forward, she rode him, perched like a naked little fairy, fluttering her wings.

After the sex was over and they lay tangled together, cooling down from their orgasms, he squeezed his eyes shut. But he couldn't shut down his mind. What if Bailey really was on the verge of loving him?

He opened his eyes, and she snuggled closer. If she loved him, then he had the capacity to destroy her, to break her heart. He skimmed a hand down her back, worrying that he wasn't good enough for her. No matter how hard he tried to make amends for being Ron's son, he still felt tainted inside. It was even worse now that he'd watched that show with Bailey, pulling him even closer to the fray.

Rather than keep quiet, he said, "I know we agreed to put the love stuff to rest. But are you positive that you're not having those types of feelings for me? I need to know for sure that it isn't going to happen."

She pulled back to glare at him. Yet in spite of her tough expression, she still looked vulnerable, somehow.

"I already told you that love isn't an issue for me," she replied.

"But just in case, I don't want to hurt you." The

way his dad had done to his mom. The comparison alone made him ill.

"There is no 'just in case.' I'm not going to fall prey to love, and you're not going to hurt me."

He was so confused that he hardly knew what to think anymore. "I'm sorry. I shouldn't have mentioned it. But you know how panicked I would be if your mother's claim was true."

"Only it's not true. She's a hopeless romantic, but I'm not like her. Love has never felt possible to me." She lifted her chin in what seemed like way too much bravado. "Besides, I just want to enjoy our affair instead of giving credence to what my mom said."

"I want to enjoy our time together, too," he replied, still struggling with the concerns he'd raised. Was she trying too hard to convince him not to worry? "But if something goes wrong—"

"Stop dwelling on this, Wade. Nothing is going to go wrong."

He forced a smile. "So, the world isn't going to come crashing down on us?"

"Not in the least." She curled up against him, snuggling in once again. "I swear, everything will be all right."

Bailey's life was spinning out of control. She hadn't seen Wade since his last visit, the fund-raiser was only a week away…and her period was late.

She hadn't made a fuss about it at first. She'd been so busy working on the ball, she'd chalked it up to stress. But this was the sixth day, and something just didn't seem right.

Was she pregnant? Was that possible? She'd been on birth control the entire time she was with Wade.

Margot was on her way over with a pregnancy test. Bailey feared that it might be too soon for an accurate reading. From what she'd read online, it was best to wait at least a week after a missed period. But Margot insisted that it was worth a shot, that six days was only twenty-four hours shy of a week.

Bailey sat on the edge of a dining room chair, waiting for Margot to hurry up and get there. What was she going to do if she was pregnant? She'd assured Wade that everything was going to be fine, and now she might be carrying his child. A complication neither of them had ever considered.

It had to be a false alarm. It didn't make sense that her birth control would've failed. As soon as Margot arrived with the test, her fears would be put to rest. Surely the results would be negative.

She got up from her chair and went into the kitchen to make a cup of mint tea. Once it was ready, she stood at the counter in her sweatpants and slippers, taking desperate little sips.

When the doorbell sounded, she set her cup down and rushed to answer it.

There was Margot, looking a bit frantic herself, with her unruly red hair in a ponytail and a white paper bag in her hand. She entered the house and said, "I got two tests. Two different brands, in case one is more accurate than the other. They both say they're good for early readings, though."

"Thank you. I'm so glad you're here. I was about ready to go out of my mind."

Margot thrust the bag at her. "Hopefully one of these will work. I can't imagine you being pregnant, not if you've been diligent with your birth control."

"I'm fanatical about it."

"Then don't worry. It'll be okay."

"That's what I keep telling myself." She clutched the bag to her chest. "Did Zeke wonder why you tore off out of the house so fast? Is he suspicious that something's going on?"

"He's working today, so he doesn't even know I'm here. Liam is with a friend, so you don't need to worry about him, either." Margot heaved a sigh. "Go on. Do this."

"Okay, but it might take me a few minutes to read the directions and decide which brand to try." She didn't want to rush the process and make a mistake.

Margot plopped down on the sofa. "I've never had cause to take one. But they seem really simple. Just pee on a stick and all that."

Bailey nodded and went into the master bathroom. She'd never expected to be doing this, and certainly not with Wade as the potential father.

She scanned both tests. They seemed similar enough for it not to matter. Either would work, so she chose the one that had been around longer, that she'd seen on TV when she was growing up.

After she was done, she recapped the device and placed it on the sink. The test had to sit for about ten minutes. She set the alarm on her phone, being as precise as possible.

She returned to Margot and said, "Even if it comes out negative, there could still be a problem if my period doesn't start soon."

"Don't start making up scenarios before they happen. Let's see what the test says and go from there."

"You're right. I need to trust the process." She scooted onto the sofa and fidgeted in her seat. The minutes ticked by.

Finally, the alarm beeped, and they both jumped up. Margot entered the bathroom with her, and Bailey approached the device.

She leaned over to read it. "Oh my stars. I think it's positive."

"You think?" Margot sounded as stunned as she felt. "Either it is or it isn't."

"The line that indicates a positive reading is really faint, so I can't be sure." She grabbed the directions again to reread them, fearing that her knees might buckle. She clutched the paper in her hand. "Even with as faint as it is, it's still considered a positive result."

Margot gestured to the unopened box on the counter. "Maybe you better take the other test to be sure."

"Thank God you got two. But I need to drink

some water. Or maybe the rest of my tea. I left it in the kitchen. It'll need to be reheated, though."

"I'll get it for you." Margot dashed off.

When she returned, Bailey was shivering. But the warm tea helped. She drank it quickly, and Margot left her alone again.

Bailey took the second test. It was starting to feel like déjà vu. Would the result be the same?

This one took a shorter amount of time. Five minutes. Was that good or bad? She didn't know.

When the time was up, Margot once again joined her to read it. Only it didn't solve anything. It came out inconclusive.

"What does that mean, exactly?" Margot asked.

Once again, Bailey consulted the package insert. "It's either one of two things—the test was faulty or it's too early to know." Bailey sat on the lid of the commode. Should she believe those faint lines on the other test? Or was that some sort of faulty reading, too? "I can't go through this again. I need to know for certain."

"It would probably be best to see a doctor," Margot said.

Bailey nodded. Problem was, it was only Saturday. She would have to wait until Monday to call to make an appointment. This was going to be the longest, scariest, loneliest weekend of her life. And now all she wanted was to be with Wade. At least they could panic together. Should she plan a trip to see him? She knew he was home, taking a few days off.

After Margot left, Bailey made the emotional decision to go to San Francisco that same night. Only she wasn't going to warn Wade that she was coming. She didn't want to worry him this soon. Once she got there, she would call him and arrange to talk in person.

Bailey took a commercial flight, but it was delayed, putting her into San Francisco at a much later hour than she'd anticipated. By now, it was nearly bedtime, and she was too exhausted and fraught with nerves to call Wade. Needing to rest, she checked into a hotel. She would contact him tomorrow when she could think clearly.

She got ready for bed and climbed under the covers, pulling them up to her neck. But all she could think about was the baby. Or the maybe baby or whatever it was.

She slept fitfully and when the morning light careened through her fifth-story window, she shot out of bed.

She checked the time on her phone: seven forty-five. She brewed a cup of coffee, giving herself a caffeine boost before summoning the strength to call Wade. She skipped room service and ate a protein bar that she'd brought with her.

She was just as nervous today as when she'd arrived yesterday. But then something happened that shook her to her core. Her period started.

Oh my God. She dug through her overnight bag

for a tampon. She always carried them in her luggage, and this trip was no exception. She dashed into the bathroom, her hands quaking.

Afterward, she sat on the unmade bed and burst into tears. She wasn't pregnant. There was no maybe baby. Her life would carry on as usual.

Then why wasn't she more relieved? Why was she still shaking and crying? Was she in shock? She wiped her tears, but she still felt empty inside. Bailey was confused. And now here she was, alone in a hotel and uncertain of what to do.

Maybe some research would help? She got on her phone, looking for a logical explanation as to why the pregnancy tests hadn't given her accurate readings.

After quite a bit of digging, she discovered that a new health supplement she'd been taking was the likely culprit, the potent herbal mixture interfering with the results of the tests.

Should she go home and try to forget the whole thing? Or should she call Wade and ask him to stop by so she could tell him her mixed-up story?

She walked over to the window, gazing out at the view. She needed to see Wade. She'd come all this way, and she wasn't going to disappear without confiding in him.

Bailey took a deep breath and dialed his number. He answered on the fourth ring.

"Hey, there," he said. "What's going on?"

"Hi." She struggled to control the quaver in her voice. "I know you didn't expect to hear from me this weekend, but I made an impromptu trip to San Francisco. I'm at the Marriott Marquis on Mission." She gave him her room number. "Will you come see me? There's something I have to tell you."

"Oh, wow. You're in town? Is everything okay?"

"Initially, I came here because I thought something was wrong, but it worked itself out." She touched her stomach. "But I don't want to go home without giving you the whole story. I need to talk to you in person."

"All right. Hang tight. I'll be there as soon as I can." He hesitated. "Are you sure you're okay?"

"Yes." Or she hoped that she was. She couldn't seem to vanquish that strange emptiness inside her.

They ended the call, and she tidied the room, making the bed, rinsing out her coffee cup and closing her luggage.

She turned on the TV, but then the noise bothered her, so she shut it back off. Was the emptiness inside her sadness? Was she mourning the loss of a baby that never even existed?

By the time Wade texted to inform her that he was in the lobby and would be right up, she thought she might faint. Pregnant women got light-headed, didn't they? Yes, but that wasn't why she felt dizzy. There was no child. Bailey was suffering from anxiety. Or grief. Or whatever it was.

She propped open the door so Wade didn't have to knock. She wanted to make his entrance into her room as simple as possible.

A few minutes later, he poked his head in. "Bailey?"

"I'm here." She stood by the entertainment center, twisting her hands together, locking her fingers, then unlocking them.

He entered the room and closed the door behind him. He wore jeans and a charcoal-colored T-shirt. His ever-changing eyes were gray, too, nearly the same deep, dark shade as his shirt. But it was his expression that struck her the most: the concern etched on his face. He was worried about her.

She was worried about herself, too. Because suddenly she knew why the loss of the fictional baby was hitting her so hard.

Bailey was in love with Wade. Frighteningly, nervously in love. Why else would she be falling apart, with an ache the size of Jupiter ripping through her heart?

She nearly pitched forward, wanting to die on the spot. She'd insisted all along that she didn't love him. She'd denied being capable of having those types of feelings. She'd even promised him that it would never happen. And now she was a liar. A big, fat, love-struck liar.

But she couldn't reveal her dilemma, not until she explained why she'd come to San Francisco in the first place.

"Do you want to sit?" she asked, gesturing to the dining table by the window.

"No, thanks. But you can, if you need to. Are you

sure you're all right?" He frowned. "You don't seem the least bit okay."

She wasn't, and especially now that she knew how she felt about him. This was her worst nightmare. It was going to be his, too. She glanced over at the table. Sitting wouldn't do her any good. Nothing would. She remained standing.

She hastily said, "I thought I was pregnant. I took two different tests. The first one was positive and the second one was inconclusive. I planned on calling my doctor on Monday, but I was too anxiety ridden to wait alone, so I came here to be with you. But then my period started, and I knew it was a false alarm."

He didn't respond. He looked instantly overwhelmed, and this was just the beginning. Once he absorbed that information, she would take the next horrific step—telling him that she loved him.

Eleven

Wade's thoughts spun. What if the pregnancy had been real and Bailey actually had been carrying his child? Would she have kept it? What kind of parents would they have been? He couldn't fathom being a father, not when his own bastard of a dad was never far from his mind.

"I'm sorry you went through that," he said, trying to offer Bailey comfort. She'd come here because she needed him, obviously. He understood that she hadn't been able to cope with the unsettling results of her tests alone. "If you had called me yesterday, I would've come to you."

"I appreciate that, but I was so anxious, I just wanted to get away. I planned on calling you last night, but my flight got in really late, so I waited until today." She clutched her middle. "And then this morning, everything changed."

"What would you have done if there had been a baby?" he asked. "How would you have handled it?"

"I would've become a single mom, I guess." Her breath hitched. "I wouldn't have expected us to get married or anything like that."

Her response made him think of his mom and how she'd struggled to raise him when he was little, before she'd gotten together with Carl. "I would've helped you, Bailey, and not just with money. I would've tried to be a good dad, even if I probably would've had a panic attack every day for the rest of my life." He expelled the air in his lungs. "I mean, what do I know about being a father?" He'd never had to devote himself to another person, to nurture them, to give them everything they needed. Being a parent was the most important job in the world, and both of his parents had failed him. As much as he loved his mom, she'd fallen apart over his dad, to the point of neglecting herself over it. She'd died far too young. "Carl was the only father I ever had, and we never really communicated the way we should've."

"I can see the fear in your eyes just talking about this." She rocked forward a little. "I'm afraid, too. But not just from the pregnancy scare. There's something else I have to tell you." She walked over to the dresser, where two bottles of water sat. She uncapped one and took a swig. She turned to face him again. "Something else that threw me for a loop."

He shifted his stance. She was making him nervous. The color even drained a bit from her face. "Just tell me." He couldn't begin to guess what was going on.

"I'm in love with you, Wade. It didn't hit me until I saw you today. I was feeling empty about the baby not being real, and then I just knew. I knew how I felt about you."

He nearly stumbled where he stood. But maybe he shouldn't be so shocked. He'd already been worried about this before, and now his concern had become a reality. "I don't know what to say. The last time I saw you, you reassured me that love wasn't part of the deal. That it would never happen. And now you…" He shook his head, his pulse beating in his throat. "What am I supposed to do now?" How was he supposed to handle it?

"What are *you* supposed to do? What about *me*? This isn't how I want to feel." Her voice broke. "It hurts, all over, everywhere."

Her fragility was too much to bear. He hated being the cause of her stress. Everything about this scenario seemed dreadfully wrong.

"I just want this feeling to go away," she said. "For it to stop hurting."

He fought his next breath. "Then maybe we should agree to end our affair. Maybe your feelings will go away if we don't see each other anymore."

It was the only solution he could think of, the only way out for both of them.

She flinched, clearly taken aback. "Really? That's your answer, to get rid of me?" She seemed angry, but a second later, she paused to study him, her expression riddled with a sudden burst of hope. "Are you sure that you're not falling in love, too? And that you're not just acting out of fear?"

Hell, yes, he was scared. He'd been troubled all along about them getting too close. "I care about you, more than I've ever cared about anyone. But I can't fall in love."

Her gaze sought his. "If you care so much about me, then what's stopping you?"

"It's just something inside me, something distant and alone." A vague response, if there ever was one. But what was he supposed to say? That he was the son of a lovesick mother and a criminal father? That sometimes when he looked in a mirror, he saw his father staring back at him? Wade didn't know how to conquer his demons and be the man Bailey needed him to be. "I wish it could be different." He took a cautious step toward her. "But I don't see how it can be."

"Then what choice do I have, except to go home and forget about you?" She lifted her chin, her tone edged with a loss that cut straight to the bone. "I can't change who you are or make you feel more than you're willing to feel."

He looked into her eyes. She was resigning to ending their affair, ending their friendship, too. Was this really the right thing to do? Or was he condemning them both to heartache? He was as lost and confused as she was.

"I'm sorry," he said. "I'm so sorry."

She didn't respond. She only stood there, as if she couldn't think beyond the moment.

He spoke softly when he said, "Whenever you're ready to go home, I can a have my pilot take you, if you don't want to go off alone." She already seemed far too lonely.

"I can take a commercial flight." She backed away from him, refusing his offer, blinking, fighting her tears. "You don't need to cater to me."

Was she going to cry after he was gone? He'd protected her when they were young, and now he was the source of her pain.

"I never meant to hurt you, Bailey."

"You told me from the beginning that you weren't wired for love. I said those things, too. It happened to me, and that's my burden to bear. But if we don't belong together, then you should leave now."

He nodded, uncertain of what else to do. He'd already caused her enough pain. He exited the room, and she closed the door, shutting him out. He stood in the hallway, wishing that he could go back inside and hold her until the hurting stopped. But he couldn't come to her rescue. Wade couldn't even save himself.

Bailey returned to LA and went straight to her mom's house. She broke down and recited the entire story, including the details about her pregnancy scare. And now she was curled up in her old bedroom, on a puffy white bed, resting her head on her mom's lap. The room had been redecorated since her youth, with none of her belongings left, yet at this distraught moment, it felt like home.

"My poor sweet girl," Mom said in a soothing voice. "Crying over a boy from the past."

"It's weird, isn't it?" Bailey dried her tears with the wad of tissue crumbled in her hand. "In high school, I used to fantasize about Wade, always wondering what kissing him would be like. He's always been part of me, somehow. But I never pictured loving him."

"I predicted that you would, but I envisioned the two of you together. That was my wish for you."

"Wade thinks my feelings for him will go away if we don't see each other anymore." She gazed up at her mother's beautifully sculpted face. "Do you think that's true?"

"Honestly, I don't know. Both of my husbands are gone, and I still love them. But maybe being widowed isn't the same as wanting someone you can't have." She stroked Bailey's hair, combing her fingers through it. "I've never been in your position. I will say this, though. You and Wade still have a chance. As long you're both still in the world, there's hope."

"Hope for what? That he'll fall in love with me, too, and that neither of us will be afraid of what the future will bring?"

"No one ever said that love was easy. But if two people are devoted to each other and if they want the same things, they can make it work."

Bailey sucked in her breath. That sounded complicated to her. So painfully complex. "Do you think I would've made a good mom…you know, if the baby had been real?"

"Yes, I absolutely do."

"Wade said that he would've tried to be a good dad. But he also said that he probably would've had panic attacks over it."

"Being responsible for another human being is scary. It used to scare the dickens out of me."

"It doesn't matter now, anyway." Bailey cradled her vacant womb. "It's not like I'll be having kids or anything else with him." She couldn't create a life with a man who'd rejected her. "I just need to try to forget that I ever loved him."

Mom heaved a heavy sigh. "You've got the fundraiser coming up to keep you busy. Hopefully that will help."

"I'm going to do my best." She sat forward, attempting to stay strong and focused, even if she wanted to sink back into the covers and cry all over again.

On the day of the ball, Bailey's heart was still hurting. If everything hadn't gotten so messed up, she would've been attending the event with Wade. But she was alone, at her house, gazing at her reflection in the closet-door mirror.

A trio of people had helped her get ready. They'd done her hair and makeup and buttoned her into her gown. The blue silk dress was from the late 1870s, with a modest neckline offering bits of lace. Ribbons and bows draped along the back of the skirt.

She fingered the antique comb in her hair, wondering if she was making a mistake by wearing it. Wade had bought it for her when they'd shopped in Haight-Ashbury when they were still together.

It was her own fault for showing it to the stylist who'd done her hair. But it did look perfect with her gown, far better than the accessories the stylist had intended to use.

Her hair was a mass of old-fashioned waves hanging behind a loose topknot. She touched the comb again. She couldn't bear to remove it, even if it did remind her of Wade. But everything reminded her of him. She couldn't get him out of her mind. Her plan to stop loving him wasn't working.

She turned away from the mirror and reached for her bag, a silk drawstring reticule that complemented her dress. At one time, this type of purse had been considered risqué because it was basically a pocket that women carried on the outside of their garments. Funny how times had changed. Fashion had come a long way. But not unrequited love, Bailey thought. It hurt no matter what century you lived in.

She took a deep breath, preparing to leave. Mom had arranged for a limo to pick her up, and it was already waiting at the curb. She would be alone in the car. Mom was arriving separately, and so were Zeke and Margot. Bailey was going early, anyway. She wanted to make sure everything was in order before the ball officially started. The event was sold out, and thanks to her mom, the guest list consisted of Hollywood's finest. No doubt Gordon would be pleased. Of course, his biggest thrill would be meeting the illustrious Eva Mitchell and having the opportunity to dance with her.

Mom intended to be a bit late, making Gordon wait for her entrance. Always the movie star, Bailey thought. But it seemed exciting. For her mother, at least. At this point, Bailey just wanted this night to end, and it had barely begun.

She rode in the long white limo, her dress fanned around her. Even with the slim silhouette of her gown, she still wore a petticoat. Some of the other women would probably have numerous petticoats beneath their skirts. Mom's custom-made gown required a crinoline, a hoop that made it exceptionally wide. The top of her dress, however, exposed more cleavage that was acceptable in Victorian times, but Mom had always been a rule breaker.

For Bailey, the lonesome drive to Pasadena felt long and grueling. She gazed out the window, summoning the strength to put on a happy face. She couldn't show up at her very first fund-raiser acting like a lovelorn fool.

Finally, she exited the limo and entered the estate where the ball was being held. The first time she'd ever been here was with Wade, when they'd checked out the property for her foundation. But that seemed like a lifetime ago. Happier times. Sexier times. She missed the warmth of his body next to hers. She missed everything about him.

Smoothing her skirt, she headed into the kitchen to see how the caterers fared. The food looked fabulous. No problems there. Next, she met with Claire, the foundation manager she'd hired, to discuss the rest of the details. Twenty-two-year-old Claire possessed a sunny personality. She even wore a bright yellow gown. While Claire assured Bailey not to worry, other members of the planning committee dashed about, doing their jobs, as well.

The ballroom was decorated in burgundy and gold, giving it a smooth, rich feel. The garden overflowed with cosmos, marigolds and dahlias. The band consisted of a piano, cornet, violin and cello.

As soon as the event was underway, guests gathered for cocktails. Gordon arrived in a velvet-trimmed tuxedo. Bailey greeted him at the door. He was quite the charmer, short and stout, with a bald head and twinkling blue eyes. She informed him that her mother was running late, but once she arrived, her dance card would be reserved exclusively for him. He seemed delighted at the news. He thanked Bailey and joined the party, socializing with the celebrities who were already there.

The next familiar face Bailey saw was Shayla Lewis, all dolled up in a pink taffeta gown. She walked in with Kirk, her loyal husband, by her side. The apologetic essay she'd written had garnered mostly positive feedback, enough to make her comfortable about being part of the fund-raiser.

Shayla and Kirk approached Bailey, and the three of them chatted about inconsequential things. Then Shayla looked around and asked, "Where's Wade? I'd like to say hello to him, too."

Bailey kept her cool, even if her heart had begun to pound. She hadn't told anyone outside her inner circle that she and Wade had been lovers, and she certainly didn't want to give herself away to her former rival.

"Unfortunately, he couldn't made it," she replied without further explanation.

"Oh, that's too bad." Shayla reached for her husband's arm. "Will you give him my regards?"

"Yes, of course." Bailey tried not to be envious of Shayla's happy marriage, but it still stung deep inside. "I hope you enjoy the ball."

"I'm certain we will. Thank you again for inviting us." Shayla and Kirk excused themselves and disappeared into the burgeoning crowd.

Soon, Margot and Zeke showed up, and Bailey was grateful to see them. Margot had donned a green gown and emerald jewels, and Zeke looked big and broad and self-assured. His company was providing security for the ball, his agents blending into the background.

Zeke offered to get Margot and Bailey a drink,

and as he headed for the bar, the women moved closer to each other.

"How are you doing?" Margot asked in a near whisper.

"I'm trying to hang on, even if I just want to rush off and cry." A lump formed in Bailey's throat. "No matter what I do, I can't stop thinking about Wade. Even Shayla asked about him."

"I keep hoping that he'll turn up and surprise you."

"And profess that he loves me? I'm supposed to be forgetting that I have feelings for him, not waiting around to be swept off my feet."

Margot reached for her hand. "I know. But it would make this night seem like a fairy tale if it happened."

"I don't believe in fairy tales. But thanks for thinking of me." She knew Margot meant well. "I just need more time to heal." A lifetime of healing, she thought. "I can't help but wonder what he's doing. He hasn't posted anything on social media since we stopped seeing each other. I wasn't even sure if I should keep following him."

"Is he still following you?"

"Yes, but I've been lying low, too, except for posts about the fund-raiser." Bailey glanced over and saw her brother returning with the drinks. She signaled for Margot to change the subject. Although Zeke knew what was going on, Bailey preferred not to discuss her broken heart in front of him.

About an hour later, their mother glided into the ballroom, making her grand entrance. Gordon turned and caught sight of her, and Bailey watched him stride across the floor to make her acquaintance. At least he was happy, meeting the woman of his dreams. Bailey feared that she was never going to dream again.

Wade had never felt so alone. There was no one to talk to, no one to call or text. At least no one he felt comfortable sharing his feelings with.

He'd spent the past week thinking about Bailey, needing her, missing her, obsessing about her every moment of the day. He'd dismissed her from his life, but that was futile. He couldn't deny that he loved her. That he'd been fighting feelings he couldn't control. He was still scared, though. That hadn't changed.

Should he go see her? Would it help to look into her eyes, to touch her cheek, to hear her voice, to tell her the truth about himself? Not just his struggle over loving her, but his struggle over his dad, too? The secret he'd been keeping. The whole sordid story.

The fund-raiser was going on now. If he engaged his pilot, he could make it to Pasadena before the ball was over. He already had his Victorian tux ready to go. His tailor had completed it before his affair with Bailey had ended. But would it be right to intrude on her special night? What if she didn't want him anymore? He feared rejection. But if he did nothing, he would never know how she felt.

He called his pilot and got the ball rolling. After that, he took a quick shower, slicked back his hair and got dressed.

He made it to the airport in record time, but the flight had to wait for clearance. He considered a drink, something strong and stiff to take the edge off. But he changed his mind, opting to keep a clear head.

Finally, the plane taxied down the runway and took off. Once they were high above the ground, Wade glanced out the window, studying the shapes of the clouds. It made him think of his mother, all wrapped up in heaven.

Was she watching over him? Did he she want him to find love, to settle down, to have a family, to quit despising his father? Wade was still so damned angry at his dad, a hatred that just wouldn't go away. And now he was on his way to see Bailey and try to undo the damage he'd done to her.

Wade arrived at LAX, with a town car waiting to pick him up. While he was in the car, he booked a suite at a hotel near the fund-raiser. He wasn't going to assume that Bailey would invite him to stay with her tonight. She deserved time to think about what he had to say.

He wasn't going to lie and say that his DNA wasn't tainted from being Romeo Ron's son. He wasn't going to pretend that he hadn't inherited some of his father's unsavory qualities. Otherwise, Wade wouldn't have become The Outlaw. He wouldn't have ditched Bailey, either. Or lied to her all this time.

He checked the pocket watch attached to his suit. At this point, he wished the ball was a masquerade so he could slip in unnoticed. He didn't want to stop and chat with other guests. He only wanted to see Bailey.

The traffic was heavy, making his car ride even more stressful. Would he spot Bailey right away or would he have to search for her amid the crowd? Would he arrive in time to ask her to dance? And if he did, would she even allow him the luxury of being his dance partner?

He had no idea what color she would be wearing or how her hair would be fixed. All he knew was that she intended to wear an authentic gown. But no matter how she was attired, he knew that she would be beautiful. She always was.

He closed his eyes for a minute, picturing her in his mind. He'd spent his entire adult life running from the idea of love, and now he was heading toward it.

He opened his eyes and blew out a breath. If the fear coiling inside him would ease up, he would feel a whole lot better. But until he connected with Bailey, his anxiety wasn't going to subside. And even then, it might not. Sometime tonight, he would be telling her exactly who Wade Butler was.

Twelve

Bailey heaved a heavyhearted sigh. The ball wasn't over, but it was nearing its close, with just a few more dances left. Her mom and Gordon continued their pairing, waltzing beautifully together. She wouldn't be surprised if they started dating for real.

Zeke and Margot had already left, eager to get home to their son. Shayla and Kirk were about to depart, too. They approached Bailey to say their goodbyes.

"It was a lovely party," Shayla said. "You and your committee did an amazing job."

"Thank you." She had to agree. The fund-raiser was a success, with plenty of money being donated to the Free Your Heart Foundation. "I'm glad you had a good time."

"We definitely did." Shayla looked past her, then widened her eyes. "Well, look who made it after all. Wade just got here."

Bailey nearly froze, afraid to see for herself. But she couldn't behave like a jilted lover. Not now. Not like this. "Really?" she asked lightly before she slowly turned around.

There he was, entering the ballroom in his tailcoat tuxedo, looking like a misty mirage. She could barely focus, her gaze blurring with tears she struggled to hold back.

Why was he here? What was his agenda? Was he hoping to renew their friendship? Or did he love her, in the achingly awful way that she loved him?

"Oh, my," Shayla said as Wade zeroed in on Bailey, and they stood across the room, staring at each other.

The jig was up, Bailey thought. Shayla could tell something was amiss. By now, Bailey's hands were quaking.

"I think we better go," the brunette said to her husband.

They walked away, passing Wade on their way out. He was still staring at Bailey. She clutched her drawstring purse, holding it a little too tightly.

He made his way over to her, and she released a shuddering breath. She hoped he didn't touch her. She wasn't ready to be touched by him. If he wasn't here to profess his love, she would only hurt worse.

And even if he did love her, that didn't mean they would live happily ever after.

"Hi," he said softly.

"Hi," she replied, not knowing what else to say.

"May I have this dance?" he asked.

She hesitated. Dancing would put them painstakingly close. But somehow, it seemed easier than talking. A way to break the ice. She just hoped that her lovesick heart could bear it.

Bailey nodded, accepting his invitation. He extended his arm and escorted her onto the dance floor.

They waltzed in silence, moving to the music. She imagined kissing him. She couldn't help but remember the taste of his lips.

"You look beautiful," he said, as if he was thinking about kissing her, too. "But I knew you would."

She thanked him, then glanced away, needing to get her bearings. He was making her dizzy.

He spoke again. "I have a lot to tell you. But we can't really talk here. I reserved a suite at the hotel down the street. Maybe when the ball is over, you can come see me, and I can say what I need to say."

She agreed that this wasn't the time or place to have a personal discussion. But heavens, she was nervous about hearing him out. "I'll meet you at your hotel later. I'll have my driver bring me."

"I haven't checked in, other than online, so I don't have my room number yet. But I'll text you as soon as I have it."

"How long are you staying at the ball? Are you leaving after this dance?"

"I was hoping to stay for the final dance. Unless this is the last one."

"There's two more after this." She looked over at her mom and Gordon. Mom had caught wind of her and Wade, too. "We can dance to both of them, if you want."

"I definitely do."

He held her a little closer, making the pulse in her neck flutter. She couldn't begin to guess what their discussion would entail. But one thing was sure— their attraction was still going strong. Her traitorous body hungered for his.

"I can't sleep with you tonight," she said suddenly. She needed to keep a level head, and she couldn't do that by climbing into bed with him.

"I'm not asking you to spend the night with me. I just want to talk."

She let out the breath she'd been holding and danced the next two waltzes with him. The final song was soft and dreamy and far too romantic, creating longings she was still trying to curb.

When the song ended, he stepped back, and in the next telltale instant, he nodded to her mother and Gordon. They returned his acknowledgment, but they didn't come over to him. Clearly, they sensed they should stay away. Or Mom certainly did.

"I should go now," Wade said. "I don't want to

intrude on you getting things wrapped up here." He leaned forward to embrace her. "I'll see you later."

The hug was warm and tender. Bailey nearly struggled to let go, but she maintained her dignity and released him.

She watched him depart, and after he was gone, she stared at the empty doorway with her pulse beating much too fast.

Wade sat across from Bailey in his hotel suite. She'd arrived not more than five minutes ago. He hadn't changed out of his tux. He'd removed his jacket, but he still wore the rest of his suit, rather than leave Bailey alone in her Victorian garb. In this setting, the old-fashioned gown gave her a ghostlike quality. Or maybe she just seemed that way. A former lover who could disappear at any moment.

"Are you sure I can't get you something to drink?" he asked.

"Yes, I'm sure." She put her hands on her lap, twining the ties on her purse.

He'd left the door to the bedroom ajar, and now he wished he'd closed it. He could easily imagine her there, strewn on the bed in her slip or chemise or whatever she had on under her gown. He noticed that the comb decorating her hair was one of the trinkets he'd given her.

Did she still love him? Even if she did, that didn't stop her from being wary. He noticed how cautious she was. But why wouldn't she be, with him showing up on the night of the ball with a story to tell?

He shifted uncomfortably in his seat, preparing to start the conversation. The room they occupied was decorated with a love seat and two overstuffed chairs. They'd both opted for the chairs.

"I lied to you before," he said. "You kept asking me if something was wrong, and I kept saying no. But there is something that's been troubling me since before my mom died. It has to do with my father. I know who he is, and although we've never actually met, I hate him with every fiber of my being."

Bailey flinched at his harsh words, but she didn't say anything. She merely waited for him to continue.

Wade got right to it. "He's the guy the press called Romeo Ron in the TV show you and I watched. I was planning on telling you that night, but I couldn't bring myself to say it then. My mom was one of his victims, but she never reported him. She was madly in love with him and kept making excuses for why he did what he did."

Bailey frowned. "Did she tell you all of this before she died?"

"No. About three months before she passed, I overheard her and Carl having a private conservation. I couldn't hear the details of what they were saying, but I could tell they were discussing my dad and some recent news they'd heard about him. Up until then, I'd assumed he was dead."

"Did they let it slip that he was a criminal?"

"No, and they didn't know I was listening, either. I didn't ask them about it. I was too scared of what the answer would be. It was obvious that Mom was upset. Later, after she died, I approached Carl. He was reluctant to tell me at first, but I kept bugging him, and eventually he gave in. He explained that my dad's picture was in the paper, and my mom recognized him. She didn't know his real name. He used an alias when he'd romanced her. But there he was, the man she'd never stopped loving, being indicted on multiple charges. He'd ripped off other women, too. But until then, my mom was under the belief that she was the only one. She'd convinced herself that he'd stolen her money for a noble reason, that maybe someone in his family was sick and he was trying to save their life. She refused to entertain the idea that he was a career criminal or a con man. She even thought he would come back someday to apologize and return her money, and then she could tell him about me. But once she saw the newspaper article, she couldn't live in her fantasy world anymore."

"Did she consider coming forward then?" Bailey asked.

Wade shook his head. "She was too hurt and ashamed."

"I'm so sorry." Her voice broke a little. "You must have been devastated when Carl told you all of that."

"It hurt beyond belief, losing my mom and then finding out about my dad. It's also what led me to take on the role of The Outlaw. I hacked in to the

FBI to become a hero, to be different from my dad and prove that I'd never be like him. But in the end, I became a criminal, too." Wade paused, tugging at his vest, wishing it wasn't so damned tight. "Sometimes I still worry that I'm like him."

"You're nothing like that. You'd never steal from anyone or take their livelihood away. It's obvious that you're the mystery benefactor from the show we watched. That you're the one who reimbursed Ron's victims."

"I shouldn't have kept so many secrets from you. You've been nothing but honest, and I've been lying to you from the start."

Her gaze latched onto his. "You're being honest now."

"Yeah, but there's more I have to tell you." He gave up the fight and unbuttoned his vest before it squeezed the life out of him. "I love you, Bailey. That's the main reason I'm here, to let you know how I feel, and to ask you if you still have feelings for me."

She caught her breath. "I do. I absolutely do. But now I'm more scared than ever. How are we ever going to be together if you have such hate in your heart for your dad? Harboring that type of negativity could destroy you even more than it already has. It could destroy us, too, and put a dark cloud over everything we do."

"Are you saying that I should forgive him?" He stood and walked over to the bar, pouring himself the drink he'd craved earlier. "I can't just let that bastard off the hook."

"By no means am I condoning what he did. But if you forgive him, then you'll be freeing yourself from the pain he caused. You'll be freeing your heart."

He downed the alcohol. "Please don't preach to me about that." He didn't need to be lectured.

"I'm trying to help you understand what you're up against. Your dad doesn't even know you exist, so what's the point of poisoning yourself over him?"

"Then maybe I should go see him and let him know I exist. Then I can hate him in person."

"That's not what I'm saying." She left her chair and came over to him, the hem of her gown trailing across the floor. "You're better than that."

"No, I'm not." He looked into her eyes. Sweet Bailey. He ached to have her, to marry her, to have babies with her. But he couldn't get past the bitterness that fueled him. He didn't want to forgive Romeo Ron.

"Please." She implored him. "Don't keep doing this to yourself."

He reached for her hand, but only for a second. Touching her wouldn't ease his pain. "You should go now. Back to the canyon and the stories you create."

She curled her fingers into her palms. "And what are you going back to?"

"The same as you," he replied. "Go back to the way I lived before." A single man, he thought, embroiled in the past. "But not until I visit my dad and toss my anger in his face." Wade loved Bailey, but he didn't know how to free the mangled pieces of his heart.

"Why did you do this?" she asked. "Why did you come here and destroy us both all over again?"

"I was just trying to tell you the truth."

She shook her head. "A truth that makes no sense, Wade. That doesn't solve a damned thing."

It was over, Bailey thought. Wade had chosen hate over love. How in the world had it come to this?

She rode home in the limo, hurting for him and aching for herself. She had a notion to see his dad, too, and tell him how much she loved his son. But she had no right to interfere.

She missed her own daddy. She wished he was here, holding her in his arms. She wasn't going to rush over to her mom's, though, or try to seek comfort there. She wasn't going to call Margot, either. It was late, and everyone needed to sleep.

She doubted that Wade would sleep. His insomnia would probably be raging tonight. No doubt hers would be, too.

Once she reached her house, the chauffeur helped her out of the car, almost as if it was a carriage of days gone by. She tipped him, and he waited until she got safely to her front door.

She went inside, filled with despair. Upon entering her bedroom, she glanced around, thinking how empty everything seemed. But it wasn't her room. The emptiness was coming from within.

She peeled off her dress, battling buttons and bows. She walked over to the mirror in her corset and petticoat. She removed the antique comb Wade had given her and released the topknot in her hair.

A coyote howled in the distance, and her pulse jumped. The coyotes reminded her of Wade, and the first time they'd made love at her house. Was she making a mistake by not supporting his anger? No, she thought. Forgiveness was the only way to be free. If Wade continued to wallow in his hatred, he would only be hurting himself. Whether or not they were together, she wanted him to be happy.

She grabbed a shawl, covered her shoulders and went outside. She turned on the fairy lights and stood on the patio, staring out at the night, steeped in sounds of the canyon.

Wade's story made her sad. His mother's heartbreak over his dad was devastating, but now the tradition continued with more pain and more heartbreak. Why couldn't Wade see the danger in that? She was grateful that he loved her, but he needed to love himself, too. Bailey was stunned that he'd likened himself to his father.

Her Wade, she thought. Her beautiful, troubled Wade. The mystery of his past had been solved. Yet she couldn't help him comes to terms with it. She'd tried, and he'd refused to listen. There was nothing left for her to do except hope that he found his way back to her someday.

Was that possible? Or was she wishing for something that would never be? Wade was lost, but so was Bailey. Lost and alone, she thought, and longing for the man she loved.

Thirteen

Aside from touring Alcatraz, Wade hadn't been in a prison since he was paroled, and it was a sickening feeling to be in a fully functioning facility again. He wanted to turn tail and run, but he didn't. He'd come this far, and he was seeing it through to the bitter end. *Bitter* being the key word. There was no effing way he was forgiving his dad. God help him, but he couldn't bring himself to do it, not even for Bailey. Instead, he was here to confront Ron, to let that bastard know just how much he hated him.

He couldn't surprise Ron with the information that he was his son. He'd been legally obligated to disclose his relationship to the inmate on the visitor questionnaire he'd submitted, an application that the inmate had to sign, too. He had no idea how Ron felt about someone claiming to be his son, but he'd agreed to see Wade.

Had Ron asked around about him? Did he have a friend on the outside who'd researched Wade? Did he suspect that Wade was the anonymous benefactor who'd helped his victims? Anyone with half a brain could figure that out by now.

After Wade emptied his pockets and placed his possessions on a conveyor belt, he passed through a metal detector. The only things he'd brought with him were his ID and keys. Two keys, to be exact, on a simple ring with no other attachments. From there, he was frisked, much in the way travelers were searched at airports.

He was lucky, he supposed, that the California Department of Corrections and Rehabilitation had approved his application at all. Depending on the circumstances, sometimes convicted felons were denied.

Once his hand was stamped, the processing was done and he was escorted to the visitors' room he'd been assigned to.

The drab gray room was equipped with small, utilitarian tables and folding chairs. Vending machines were available, offering drinks and snacks, but only with the use of tokens. He felt sorry for the kids who were here to see their fathers. But in a creepy way, he was one of those kids. Or an adult version, anyway.

Wade took a seat and waited. As much as he wanted to yell at his old man, he was going to have to keep his cool. The last thing he needed was to create a scene. But he was still going to get his point across. He wasn't going to let Romeo Ron sit across him, acting like they were long-lost buddies.

Anxious, he glanced over at one of the guards, a baby-faced guy about his own age. He knew better than to let the guard's boyish appearance fool him. This place wasn't a playground.

A short time later, the inmates began filing into the room. Wade sat ramrod straight, scanning the men for his dad.

When he didn't see him, he started to worry. Had Ron changed his mind? Was he standing Wade up and having the last laugh?

Then he spotted Ron walking casually into the room. He had an easy vibe, a naturally charming demeanor. But that was part of his con. He even smiled at everyone he passed.

He came over to Wade, and they stared at each other. Minimal contact—a hug, a brief kiss, a handshake—was permitted at the beginning and end of a visit, but there was no way Wade was touching him.

"So here we are," Ron said while he settled into his seat.

Yeah, there they were. They looked more alike in person than they did in pictures. Ron was tall and athletically built, with graying brown hair and striking features. He'd just turned fifty-five last month, making him a savvy twenty-two-year-old when he'd screwed over Wade's mom.

"How did it make you feel when I submitted my application and said that I was your son?" Wade asked, sending him a cold look.

"Honestly? I was relieved. I've known about you for years, and I've always wanted to meet you."

Wade shook his head. "That's bullshit." He was trying to pull a con. "You didn't have a clue I existed. You probably barely even remember my mom."

Ron blew out a sigh. "I remember her well. Ginny Butler. She was as sweet as they come. But it wasn't your mom who told me about you, it was Carl."

"Yeah, right." It was obvious that Ron had done his homework, unearthing info about Wade's stepdad. "I'm not going to fall for this crap."

"It's the truth. Carl came to see me after your mom died and after you were incarcerated for that Outlaw stuff. Carl was sick then, and he knew he was dying, but he didn't want to hold his illness over you. He wanted you to accept his phone calls and visits without having to play the cancer card."

Wade got a chill, all the way down his spine. Was this story real? Had Carl reached out to Ron? "Why would he confide in you?"

"Because he suspected that someday you were going to seek me out. That you'd want to confront the man who hurt your mom. He warned me not to reach out to you, but to let you come to me. I just didn't think it would take this long. I'm impressed with how successful you are now. I knew right away that it was you who'd reimbursed my victims."

"If you knew, then why didn't you blow my cover and tell anyone?"

"Because I didn't want to mess up your life. Carl told me that your mom loved me right up until she died. Believe it or not, I loved her, too. I didn't intend to feel anything for her, but she got the best of me."

Wade lifted his eyebrows. "You loved her so much, you ripped her off? Come on, Romeo Ron, what kind of lies do you expect me to believe?"

His dad rubbed his hands across his face. "I deserve that, I do. But just so you know, she was my first mark. My uncle found her. He was in the salon where she worked getting his hair cut by another stylist when he heard your mom talking about the money she'd inherited. He came back and told me about her. He said that she seemed sweet and naive and would probably fall for me in an instant. I was drowning in gambling debts and needed a way out."

After a slight hesitation, he added, "My uncle helped me create the con. He was more a gigolo than a romance scammer. He would get rich ladies to pay his way, without having to steal from them. But in this case, he suggested that I do something drastic before the loan sharks came after me."

Wade squinted at his dad. "When did this supposed love of yours occur? When did you start feeling something for her?"

"Pretty early on. I wasn't even sure if I could go

through with the con. But then I realized that I was no good for her anyway. I lived a bad life with my uncle. A hard, angry life, and my feelings for your mother were scaring me. It was easier to just take her money and disappear than to stick around and try to deal with my affection for her. Later, I stole from other women, too. It became a lifestyle. I chose women similar to your mom because I needed a reminder of her. But I made deliberate mistakes. I did things that I knew would get me caught. I've pretty much done whatever I could to punish myself. I've never even applied for parole."

Wade wanted to believe his father's story, at least for his mother's sake, but he was still leery. "I came here to tell you that I hate you. But now I don't know what to think. You're a skilled liar, so how am I supposed to react to all of this?"

"You can check out my story. There's a record that Carl came to see me all those years ago. You can also verify that I've never applied for parole."

"Yeah, I can check on those things. But I can't check to see if your feelings are real."

"You just have to go with your gut. But for what it's worth, I really am sorry for the pain I caused. Your mother was a nice lady, and Carl seemed like an upstanding guy, too. You should have been his son, not mine." Ron glanced away. "I don't blame you for hating me."

By now, Wade could barely breathe. Should he give his dad the benefit of the doubt? Or walk away and never come back? "There's a woman I care about who wants me to forgive you. She says it's the only way I'll be free. We used to be romantically involved, but things are over between us now."

Ron looked up. "Because of me?"

"No. Because of me." He gazed across the table at his father. "I made some bad choices, too." And now he was going to make the right ones. "This is tough for me, but I'm going to do my best to forgive you. I can't keep living the way I am. I need to purge the anger and hate and win back the woman I love." He needed Bailey. He needed her so damned much. He just hoped that she still needed him, too. That he hadn't hurt her beyond repair.

His dad smiled a little. "I'm glad you're headed down a good path. Do you think you'll ever come back to see me again, or is this it? Should we say goodbye?"

"I'll come back." Walking away wasn't the answer, not if he was truly going to forgive this man. "It might take some time, but we can work on getting to know each other better. I think it's what my mom would've wanted." Her and Bailey. The two most important women in Wade's heart.

Ron waited a beat before he said, "The public might find out that I'm your dad now that you disclosed it on your application. It might get leaked to the press. Are you going to be able to handle that?"

"Yeah, I can handle it." Especially if he had Bailey by his side. He was going to see her today, just as soon this prison visit was over. Wade had no choice but to cling to hope. For him, Bailey was all that mattered.

Bailey headed home from the corner market, carrying a recycled bag filled with fresh produce. She'd walked to the store, needing some exercise and air.

Her phone had gone off in her purse, pinging with a text notification, but she couldn't shift everything to check it. She would do that later, after she settled in. She still had about twenty minutes to go. The rest of the way was long and narrow. She lived at the top of her hill.

She stopped to drink some water and carried on. She hadn't been on a walk in a while. She and Margot used to hike through the canyon when they lived closer. But Margot resided at the beach now, and it wasn't as easy for them to get together.

Once Bailey reached her street, she rounded the corner to her house. The closer she got, the faster her heart beat. And then she spotted Wade, sitting on her porch steps. The man she missed with all her might. Her lost friend and former lover.

She moved closer, and he stood and dusted off his pants. Her heart was beating triple time now, pounding clear into her throat.

He spoke first. "You didn't answer the door, so I assumed you weren't home. But then you didn't respond to my text, and I got worried that you didn't want to see me. But I had to stay and wait for you, just in case."

She held up her bag. "I walked to the store. I was going to check my texts after I got home. I'm not avoiding you." She wanted to run straight into his arms, but she didn't know why he was here. Was he delivering good news, bad news, uncertain news? "Do you want to come in?"

He nodded, and she unlocked her door. They crossed the threshold. He followed her into the kitchen so she could put her produce away, but he stood back, giving her space. She didn't want the space. She wanted him.

"Where should we sit?" she asked.

"How about the patio? I like it out there."

"Me, too." It was the first place they'd kissed. The place she still visited when she couldn't sleep.

Before they proceeded to the patio, she removed a sparkling water from the fridge and offered it to him. She already had her water.

He accepted the drink, and they went outside and sat in the rustic wooden chairs that faced the garden. The chairs were new. She'd found them at a garage sale. She'd been shopping a lot lately, buying things to try to fill the void of missing him. But nothing worked. She missed him every moment of every emotionally grueling day.

He opened the bottle and took a swig. Was he as nervous as he seemed? She was beyond nervous.

They almost seemed like strangers, gazing out at the yard in silence.

Then he said, "I went my see my dad today. That's where I was before I came here." He shifted to look at her. "But it didn't turn out like I thought it would."

She met his gaze, anxious for him to continue. "What do you mean?"

He rocked forward in his chair, reciting the things his father had told him. He ended with, "I don't know if I believe everything he said. I want to, but I can't be sure if he's trying to con me. I do plan to check out as much of his story as I can. It's probably true that Carl visited him. It would be foolish for him to make up something like that."

Bailey offered her opinion. "It makes sense in a weird way that Carl went to see him, especially if Carl thought you might try to connect with Ron someday. As for your dad..." She considered the years Ron had already spent in prison. "I think he's being truthful. What would be the point of him lying to you after all this time? If he wanted to take advantage of you or mess with your emotions, he could've done it before now. But he didn't do anything except wait to see if you ever reached out to him."

"Yeah, but do you believe the part about him loving my mom? He could've just said that to make himself seem like less of a predator."

"Love is complicated, Wade. So yes, I think it's extremely possible that he loved her." She knew firsthand how torturous love could be. "I've been scared of it my entire life and so have you. We haven't been normal in that way."

"Not in the least. But I forgave Ron. I did what you suggested. I chose love over hate. I'm going to try to have a relationship with my dad, to let it build and see where it goes." He dragged a hand through his hair, pushing it away from his face. "But I have a lot to be sorry for, too. Not with Ron, but with you. I hurt you, Bailey. I walked away from you, not once, but twice." He paused, his voice rough and shaky. "I'm an idiot for ending what we had. I love you more than I can say, more than I ever thought possible."

Tears rushed to her eyes. "I love you, too."

He softened his voice. "Will you forgive me? Will you take me back?"

"Yes." God, yes. She wasn't going to punish him for the past, and especially not after the leap of faith he was taking with his dad. "I hoped that you'd find your way back to me." It was what she'd longed for, what she needed. She got out of her chair and climbed onto his lap, curling up against him.

He held her, nuzzling her neck, keeping her close. She lifted her face, and his lips sought hers. They shared a warm and tender kiss.

Afterward, he said, "I want to marry you and have babies and do all the stuff that crazy-for-each-other couples are supposed to do. I have no idea where we're going to live or what sort of compromises we'll have to make, but I want a future with you."

"I want all of that, too." She wanted everything

with him. "We'll figure out the details as we go. Just like you're going to do with your dad."

"Ron asked me if I'd be okay if the press found out that he was my father. I assured him that I could handle it. But now I'm thinking that I should be the one to announce it. Maybe I could write an essay on your blog, revealing my story. I've never spoken publicly about being bullied as a teen or how it impacted me becoming The Outlaw. When I took on that persona, I was grieving for my dead mom and raging against the criminal dad I never knew. The dad I'm going to try to get to know now."

Bailey touched Wade's jaw, skimming her fingers along his beard stubble. "I would be more than happy to publish your essay and let you to speak your truth. I want you to free your heart in any way you can."

"I already feel free, just being here with you. You taught me the importance of love and forgiveness, and it's a lesson I'm never going to forget."

She smiled. "Look at us, being all calm and normal instead of scared and edgy."

"Yeah, look at us." He leaned down to kiss her again, proving how amazing calm and normal could be.

Wade spent the night at Bailey's, and in the daylight, they lounged lazily in bed.

"This is how Sunday mornings should be," he said. She looked sweetly tousled from their lovemaking last night, with her messy ponytail and sleepy blue eyes. "I could do this forever."

"You are going to be doing it forever." She climbed on top of him, breath to breath, limb to limb. "This is our life now."

"And what a life." He slid his hands down the sides of her naked body. He was bare, too, and getting hard. "Damn, but you have an insatiable appetite."

"Look who's talking." She rubbed against him, making him harder. "You're rapacious, too."

"Rapacious?" He moaned his pleasure. "Who uses words like that?"

She smiled, a bit too devilishly. "The writer you're going to marry."

"More like the writer I'm going to ravish." He could toss fancy R-words around, too. He switched their positions, taking the lead. He wanted to sink lusciously into her.

She didn't protest. She opened her thighs, inviting him inside. He entered her, as deeply as he could, rocking his hips and creating a sinuous rhythm.

She arched her back, and they devoured each other with heat and hunger, with love and commitment, with everything building inside them. They practically tore the bed apart in their haste, pulling and tugging, kissing and biting. Her mass of hair broke free from its ponytail, spilling loose. He grabbed handfuls of it. He loved how wild and silky it was. Nothing compared to being with her.

Wade was lost, all the way around. He belonged to her, body and soul. But she was everything he wanted.

She came first, shuddering, with her legs wrapped possessively around his waist. Desperate to join her, he let himself fall, his orgasm as powerful as hers.

He collapsed on top of her, and she held him, running a hand down his spine. He sucked in his breath, and she sighed.

Finally, he lifted his body from hers and lay next to her, letting the air cool his skin. She cooled down, too, stretching like a contented cat.

After a long silence, he said, "I think I should sell my place and move back to LA instead of you moving in with me or us dividing our time between two homes." He shifted onto his side, studying her amid the mess they'd made out of the bed. "Maybe I can buy the property behind yours and build a house that we can share. Then you can keep this one as your writing studio."

She leaned on her elbow. "That would be ideal for me, but are you sure you're ready to return to LA? Won't it affect your work?"

"I can work from anywhere. It doesn't have to be from San Francisco." He'd always been a freelance entrepreneur. "I left Los Angeles because I was running away from the stuff that happened to me here. But I'm getting past that now."

"That sounds perfect. I'll look into who owns the property behind me, and you can contact a land agent to see if you can negotiate a deal. If that lot isn't available, I'm sure you'll find something else close by."

"That works for me. I'm eager to get things going."

"Me, too. In fact, we should host a dinner tonight to celebrate our plans. I can invite my family, and we can tell them that we're going to make a life together. I'm sure that my mom will be thrilled. Margot and Zeke, too."

"Okay, let's do that." Wade was all for it. "I can also tell them about my dad. But you know what else I think we should do this week? We should build your tree house."

She broke into a grin. "Can Liam help us? It might be fun to have a kid onboard."

"Sure." He returned her grin. Someday they were going to have other kids onboard, children of their own, a family neither of them had ever known they wanted. But life was full of surprises, and he intended to enjoy every unexpected moment with the woman who'd helped restore his heart.

* * * * *

*If you loved Bailey and Wade,
don't miss
Margot and Zeke's story,*
Hollywood Ex Factor,
*part of the
LA Women duet
by Sheri WhiteFeather.
Available exclusively from
Harlequin Desire.*